THE
BOOK CENSOR'S LIBRARY

BOTHAYNA AL-ESSA

THE
BOOK CENSOR'S LIBRARY

Translated from the Arabic by
Ranya Abdelrahman & Sawad Hussain

RESTLESS BOOKS
NEW YORK · AMHERST

Copyright © 2023 Bothayna Al-Essa
Translation copyright © 2024 Ranya Abdelrahman and Sawad Hussain

First published as حارس سطح العالم by Takween Publishing House (Kuwait) and ASP Arabic (Beirut), 2019

First Restless Books paperback edition April 2024

Paperback ISBN: 9781632063342
Library of Congress Control Number: 2023945244

Quotations from *Zorba the Greek* reprinted from Nikos Kazantzakis, trans. Carl Wildman, *Zorba the Greek* (New York: Simon & Schuster, 1996)

Quotations from *1984* reprinted from George Orwell, *1984* (Boston: Mariner Books Classics, 2017)

Permission to paraphrase from *Fahrenheit 451* by Ray Bradbury granted by Don Congdon Associates Inc., on behalf of Ray Bradbury Literary Works LLC

This book is made possible by the New York State Council on the Arts with the support of the Office of the Governor and the New York State Legislature.

This book is supported in part by an award from the National Endowment for the Arts.

Cover design by Joy Richu
Interior illustrations by Mohammed Al Mohanna
Set in Garibaldi by Tetragon, London

Printed in the United States

1 3 5 7 9 10 8 6 4 2

RESTLESS BOOKS
NEW YORK · AMHERST
www.restlessbooks.org

CONTENTS

THE
BOOK CENSOR'S
LIBRARY

The events of this story happen sometime in the future, in a place that would be pointless to name, since it resembles every other place.

At all times, we must stay on the surface of language.

The surface!

Beware of wading into meaning. Do you know what happens to people who sink into meaning?

An eternal mania strangles them and they're left unfit to live.

You are a guardian of surfaces. The future of humanity depends on you.

THE FIRST CENSOR

A MAN DANCING
ON AN ISLAND

1

AS THE BOOK CENSOR awoke one morning, filled with others' words, he found himself transformed into a reader.

Lying on his back, he felt a stiffness in his neck; when he raised his head ever so slightly, he could see hundreds of books surrounding his bed, books he had no recollection of bringing home. One or two of them, certainly, but somehow the books appeared to have multiplied overnight, sprouting, dividing down the middle, copulating even. Piled up, one atop the other, towering over him, hemming him in from every side.

He remembered somewhat foggily that the books had thrown his wife out. But was that yesterday or yesteryear? Her spot in their bed was empty. Somewhere in his memory, he recalled that she had left the bed, her face red with rage, because of a forgotten book under the covers that had knocked her elbow. How accurate this was he wasn't entirely sure; more likely than not, the book had bitten her.

He didn't remember much of what had happened, akin to when an addict comes to their senses. Nighttime was the worst.

Because of his new job, he knew about the maladies caused by books—in fact, he had started to display some of the symptoms: metaphors cropping up in his head; persistent ache in his upper back; stealing books involuntarily; compulsive late-night reading by candlelight even when the power went out. One look and it was clear he had a problem: dark circles, excessive weight loss, pallid skin, bloodshot eyes, migraines, shoulder and neck pain, not to mention being more prone than others to all kinds of dark thoughts, as if he had been sentenced to forever seeing the glass half empty. He knew if he peeked inside his own head he'd find worry, depression, fury at the world. Of course he knew the signs—he'd taken an oath to avoid them when he filled out the safety and security procedures compliance form.

What he did remember from last night was his wife yelling at him to choose: the books or her. With her pillow under her arm, her eyes welling, she could barely believe it when he put his hands up to his mouth and whispered, "I can't."

"You've lost your mind!" she hissed.

And then she was gone. What had happened next? What had he done the whole night? Had he slept? Had he read?

The door slamming. Left alone with the books. He'd been scared but hadn't wanted to reveal how vulnerable he was. He knew things his wife wouldn't believe, things the other censors didn't yet appreciate. Books could hear, bite, multiply, have sex. They had sinister protocols to take over the world, to colonize and conquer—word by word, line by line, poisoning the world with meaning. But he was meant to only skim the surface of language. He thought he'd had enough training to sidestep the hazards of the job. The image of the First Censor drumming the table came to mind, his words unforgettable: *All language is smooth. There are no ripples. Stay on the surface, and you'll be the best censor.*

He hadn't understood a whit of it. Language is smooth? What did the First Censor mean by ripples? But of late he'd grown to understand. He'd started spending nights climbing mountains and wading through swamps, sometimes falling down holes to the bowels of a secret world. Language was no longer confined to the surface. But if he shared what he thought, he'd be branded a heretic, delusional. He didn't want to come across as out of control. A newly appointed censor couldn't be defeated from the start. What would people say?

It had begun with one book. He tried to recall the dream, feeling its delicate membrane enveloping him like an embryo. He had been on an island, walking barefoot along a golden shore of smooth seashells, the sea roaring. He came across a discarded book in the sand. Heavy, he needed both hands to pick it up, and found beneath it a dozen tiny crabs waving their pincers in his face. Then one after the other they began to melt back into the sand, burying themselves as if they never existed. One crab pinched his leg, waking him up. He found himself in a room that was no longer just his room, for he wasn't alone anymore but faced a beast of countless books, a book-beast that wanted to swallow him whole.

Setting his feet on the floor, he trod on book covers that were so numerous they could have covered the surface of the earth, searching for gaps on his way to the bathroom. He extended his leg toward another gap and steadied himself with his arms out wide, waving them around as if wading through a bog. Upon reaching the door, he opened it and poked his head through: his wife had left for work and taken the child to school. He was relieved to not have to face her that morning.

He splashed his face with water and rubbed his cheeks, hoping to remove the traces of the words he'd read. He had changed. He had the look of a reader—his gaze appeared to have turned in on itself.

2

The new censor was late to his office. He had stood too long, rooted to the ground in front of the Censorship Authority building, trying to guess the number of floors it contained. A few meters from the entrance, counting on his fingers, he was certain there were at least thirty-six floors. But the elevator only listed thirty.

He had heard a rumor about secret floors in government offices. They were reserved for the higher-ups, filled with computers, smartphones, and tablets. In these rooms, they accessed in secret what was called the internet. But this was just a rumor, and he knew what experts said about rumors: they were the vestige of a biological instinct to invent stories, a primitive instinct from the Old World, in the process of being wiped out.

The Censorship Authority building was a gray cube, its windows squeezed too close together and overlooking the

13

main road. To one side was a parking lot where cars could also be charged. On the other side was a garden that no one paid much attention to, a grassy patch of land bordered by bougainvillea bushes and oleander. He sighed, staring at it all, still unbelieving of his bad luck.

After long months of waiting and living on unemployment, the call had come from the employment office informing him of the book censor post. It wasn't the job he wanted. If he was fated to work for the Censorship Authority, he would have preferred to be at the Inspection Bureau. But refusing it meant waiting for who knows how much longer, barely scraping by. He couldn't do that to his wife, who was burned out from being the sole breadwinner.

Authority personnel in khaki pants and starched shirts took hurried steps to the entrance. The hallways teemed with employees. An aroma of coffee mingled with the acrid fumes of floor disinfectant. There was another elusive smell that wound its way through the building—maybe he was the only one who noticed. He guessed someone had forgotten to wash their socks or that a glass of water had spilled on the carpet somewhere. Something must have happened, leaving behind a chicken-coop-boiled-cabbage-damp-socks sort of smell.

Even the rabbits had arrived before him. He came across two in the hallway and tried to kick them, but they were always too quick. White devils! They defecated all over the place; he spotted at least three sets of droppings that had escaped the janitor's broom. He imagined the rabbits were leaving behind little tokens of love, doomed souvenirs to remind humankind, forgetful by nature, that their organizations were always susceptible to penetration. He yelled at the janitor to sweep up the filth. Spewing profanities, he entered the department and sat in his chair. Instead of inspecting a book, he placed one leg atop the other and surveilled the other seven censors.

He thought of the first day he'd arrived here for work, appointment letter in hand. I'm the new censor, he had said. They all greeted him with a nod. From the outset he noticed an inconceivable synchronization in their actions, as if they were septuplets. Aside from their work uniform, each of them wore spectacles and was balding. Like wooden dolls in a puppet theater, their invisible strings controlled by a faceless man, each censor would turn a page at the same time. Blink in unison. Scratch their noses at once. Stretch out their hands to reach for a pen, then suddenly start writing, completely in sync. They would pick up their reporting notebooks and record violations from each title. Sometimes one of them would sneeze and the rhythm that linked them would be broken. He asked himself if he too would one day be part of this collective harmony, part of the whole. But up until this very moment, he had been unable to oppose even one book.

He stared at the wall before him, at the drawn-up task schedule. The schedules were updated several times a day, so everyone knew, at any given moment, who was reading what.

The process was akin to entering a minefield or a jungle full of snakes. A rope should have been attached to each of their backs, he thought, just in case a censor lost their way back to the surface.

It was a large room, big enough for all of them. Each sat at his own desk, a crate full of books awaiting inspection at his feet. Nothing eye-catching, except for the schedule on the wall: each censor had two columns next to their name, one for the books they had finished inspecting and another for the books they were ordered to inspect. The column next to his name was empty except for one book.

It had taken him a while to grow familiar with the preventative measures that censors took to limit the impact a book had on them. At first, he thought it was a lack of professionalism, but he soon learned that everything had a reason. Anxious that the censors might wade too deep into the forest of language and lose their footing in reality, the First Censor, for example, would intentionally cough at certain times when the room grew too quiet. Sometimes he would sneeze, just so everyone would say, "Bless you!" At other times he would grumble about the heat or some other mundanity to interrupt their train of thought. He encouraged each of them to discuss what they were reading, and he would gently swat away any intrusive thoughts. The most valued behavior was to mock what one was reading—whether the book was banned or permitted made no difference. What mattered was your ability to belittle the enemy.

This was what had happened with a poetry collection the day before. "Look here!" the Second Censor cried. "Listen to this:

The sun said
Embrace me
And give me a drink from your forearm."

He then extended his left arm and began to massage it as if milking an udder. The rest of the censors laughed too loudly and took it a step further, one of them milking his own foot, another pretending to pour water from his ear. When they reached more intimate places, the First Censor scolded their improper behavior, especially with women in the building. Then someone said one could no longer tell the difference between poetry and nonsense, that literary taste was lost, to the point that everyone began wondering: what sort of book was this? By the time their conversation ended, the book had lost all value. Not just the book in question but every other book in the room. Grumbling, they returned to their inspection, more wound up than before.

But such tactics didn't work for him. He didn't understand why he couldn't, even for a moment, hate the book he held between his hands.

3

NOTHING HAD BEEN the same since he picked up the book with the blue cover.

Before he began to read, he wanted to be a bookstore inspector. Inspectors lived the good life: elegant blue uniforms, military-grade benefits, and a one percent increase in their electricity quota. Police and army club memberships would have meant entertainment perks for his daughter and discounts at most shops. Most importantly, inspectors didn't have to punch a clock when they arrived at work. All they had to do, when they received a complaint about some book or other, was visit the store in question and seize the book. And if an inspector were to find more contaminated books while there, he could live the thrill of calling the police. Nothing more exciting than watching handcuffs get slapped onto a bookseller's wrists and seeing the bookstore's doors sealed with red wax.

The Censorship Authority took the view that an inspector spent more time in the line of fire than a censor. An inspector had to deal with the likes of booksellers, book pirates, and readers. Rumor had it that these were a vicious and unruly lot who had no respect for the law, particularly those who belonged to opposition cells known as The Cancers. It was said that the blood of Old World intellectuals ran through their veins, that they were remnants of a bygone civilization, enemies of the future.

The seven censors hated inspectors because they got all the glory. *They* reaped the fruits of long hours spent inspecting books, and *they* were ultimately honored for protecting society from imminent harm. But what about the dangers a censor had to face alone? What if a book swallowed him? What about his ongoing exposure to poisonous thoughts? What if he were to become entrapped by a novel and left unfit to live in the real world?

The problem—back then—was that the new censor hadn't known someone who knew someone who knew someone else who could get him assigned to the Inspection Bureau. It took connections, and he was naive. Defenseless even. He had always felt himself to be so. Now look where that left him: full of bitterness at the thought of having to work like this—five days a week, six hours a day—in the grip of these devilish creatures with their slippery surfaces and endless traps.

And the rabbits. Why was the department full of them? The first time a rabbit bobbed up in front of him, he'd pointed at it and shouted, "Rabbit! Rabbit!"

The censors had laughed at him. "Come on—what if a lion had walked in?" But he didn't understand. Why do they let rabbits in here? Today a rabbit and tomorrow God only knows what. A cow or even a donkey might barge in. That's all we need!

"How did it get in here?"

The censors pointed to the window. "The garden next door."

Why didn't the government do anything about them? What if they spread some kind of influenza? A traditionalist, he believed that rabbits belonged in one of two places: a slaughterhouse or a bowl of broth.

Suddenly, the seven censors picked up their pens and hurled them at the rabbit. Beset by the onslaught, the animal rose up on its hind legs and turned to leave. Before it disappeared, he was certain the rabbit had singled him out. It glared at him. But the other censors told him he was imagining things.

With trembling fingers, he opened the book again. He had read this page at least ten times over. He didn't know why he was stuck on it.

The First Censor cleared his throat. "Have you finished your report yet?" he asked. "The Department Head is getting worried."

He found himself being evasive. "Actually, I've started writing it, but I don't want to skip a single line, you know?"

"You're running very late with this."

"I'll turn in my report at the end of the day."

He'd raised suspicions; everyone was wondering if he'd be able to come back from the book unscathed. The effects of the words he had read must be showing clearly on his face, or they would soon enough. The bumps and bruises were invisible, but painful nonetheless.

Opening his reporting notebook, he pretended to work on his report, but began scrawling lines he'd memorized from the book instead, as if he were trying to understand them. He imagined himself sitting on the beach, where a hulk of a man sat cross-legged in front of him, like Sinbad the Sailor, asking, *Eh friend, you have a soul, don't you?*

He shook his head. He blinked several times. It was dangerous for him to fall prey to visions, especially here. Visions, like old myths of creation, folk stories, daydreams, sexual fantasies and nonsexual ones too, were all toxic remnants of the Old World. He learned this during his training, when the First Censor explained how it all worked. He had learned that language should be an impenetrable surface. It should be smooth and flat with no bottom where meaning could settle. It was a censor's job to curb imagination.

"I found fifteen violations in three pages!" one of the censors let out triumphantly.

"What luck!"

The seven censors searched for violations as if digging for diamonds. At first, he didn't understand. Why such jubilation? One infraction was enough to ban the book and be done with it. But they told him that finding a thousand violations per year would earn him a bonus, which was the same as getting a five percent increase in his electricity quota for two months. He was confident that the book in his hands would breach the rules a hundred times over, but he still felt hesitant. Rather, he was simply unable to do it.

He went back to writing in his reporting notebook, determined to finish the job properly.

Page 117, Line 16: OFFENDS PUBLIC MORALS.

He moved to the next line. It's not that hard, he kept telling himself, not hard at all. Only, as a guardian of surfaces, it upset him to read the next sentence: *All objects in this world have hidden meanings*. He felt a sudden dryness in his mouth. The line blatantly contradicted the Censorship Authority's philosophy.

Perhaps the First Censor had been right. He had started reading before completing his training, even though he'd studied *The Manual for Correct Reading* several times over. He was sure he'd understood everything in it, but a certain something eluded him. Language was *not* a smooth surface—it was a roller coaster, a sponge, a gateway. But nobody here shared his opinion. His fellow censors would say that what could not be found on the surface wasn't there at all. When the System denied the existence of a certain idea, that was because it didn't exist.

According to *The Manual for Correct Reading*, censors must "consider words and formations in pure isolation and avoid all ideas and interpretation." All he had to do was list the offending lines in the reporting notebook, lines which fell into the forbidden trinity of God, government, and sex. All prohibitions revolved around this trinity.

At first, he'd thought the other censors were exaggerating, trying to ascribe undue importance to a simple task.

Once he'd completed a short quiz on the contents of the guide, the First Censor had given him a list of lines chosen from several books and asked him to determine whether any of them violated the rules. After passing this test, he became a novice censor in training, and was given ten books to inspect.

It seemed easy enough, and it was, in the beginning.

NO.	QUOTATION

1. If children, too, suffer horribly on earth, they must suffer for their fathers' sins, they must be punished for their fathers, who have eaten the apple.

2. As Gregor Samsa awoke one morning from uneasy dreams, he found himself transformed in his bed into a gigantic insect.

3. The Arab world is a geopolitical term that refers to a geographical area with a common history, language, and culture.

4. The daemon replied, "Yet you, my creator, detest and spurn me, thy creature, to whom thou art bound by ties only dissoluble by the annihilation of one of us."

5. All tasks are now performed using applications and information systems on the internet.

6. and two soft breasts, white like an ivory bowl kept safeguarded from any wandering hands

7. Man's warlike instincts are ineradicable--therefore a state of pure peace is unthinkable.

8. Get away, Satan, for you have been stripped of all powers. There is nothing here for you, in the presence of this pure and Holy Spirit.

9. Half-hearted or insincere apologies are often worse than not apologizing at all.

10. Democracy is the process by which people choose the man who gets the blame.

Explain the reason for the violations, if any, in the quotations shown in the table below.

SOURCE	VIOLATION / NON-VIOLATION	TYPE OF VIOLATION
THE BROTHERS KARAMAZOV Dostoevsky	VIOLATION	Refers to old beliefs, unsanctioned by the Religious Law Oversight Committee
METAMORPHOSIS Kafka	VIOLATION	Contradicts logic
GEOGRAPHY OF THE ARAB WORLD	VIOLATION	Refers to the history of the Old World.
FRANKENSTEIN Mary Shelley	VIOLATION	Transgresses against the Divine Being
THE FUTURE OF INFORMATION SYSTEMS Dr. Goran Gutshall	VIOLATION	Uses the word "internet"
Amr ibn Kulthum's Mu`allaqah	VIOLATION	Offends public morals
THE PSYCHOLOGY OF NAZISM Carl Jung	VIOLATION	Contradicts government lab results
THE SIMPLIFIED BOOK OF PRAYER	VIOLATION	Wording of the prayer is not sanctioned by the Religious Law Oversight Committee
THE LAST LECTURE Randy Pausch	NON-VIOLATION	-------------
LECTURES Bertrand Russell	VIOLATION	Threatens public order

EXAMINER'S
SIGNATURE:

4

AT FIRST, they had given him pedestrian texts.

They had titles along the lines of *A Woman's Tears*, *Your Heart is Mine*, *Because I Love You*, all of which gave him acid reflux. He wondered if it wouldn't be better to protect humanity from boredom instead, to stand up to the tidal wave of sentimentality flooding the world while no one was looking. Lately, every time he read the word "confession" or "soulmate" or "spark," he would start to itch and scratch all over his body. The Censorship Authority shouldn't have to put up with the tiresome outpourings of the heartsick. He decided it made more sense for lovers' tiffs to be handled privately, or at the Family Reconciliation Bureau. Definitely not in public, because that sort of thing was improper, not to mention dreadfully dull. And even though he had never been interested in the environment, the thought of all those trees being turned into such pointless books made his blood boil.

He stared at the pages of one such book, hoping to spot even one moment of indecency, anything to justify banning it. Finding nothing, he scanned it again and discovered a single, measly line. With his index finger on the offending sentence—"I long for you with every cell in my body"—he headed for the First Censor's desk.

"Is there any sexual innuendo in this line?" he asked.

The man shook his head knowingly. "No. Remember: only the words and formations in pure isolation."

"But 'cells,' they're everywhere. Here, here, and—" He looked behind him to make sure his colleagues weren't paying attention and pointed to his groin. "*Here*!"

The First Censor laughed. "We do *not* interpret."

He pursed his lips. Was *this* what it meant to be a guardian of surfaces? He had thought the job would be more interesting. What was the point, then, of guarding superficialities if the whole world was nothing *but* superficial? With a sigh, he went back to his desk and wrote in the reporting notebook that the book was approved. More books fit for circulation. For crying out loud!

Then he read some of the other books. He thought they ought to be banned too. Each one focused on success, money, love, happiness, as though a person could achieve these things by sheer willpower. It galled him to be told by a book that he was not a product of his circumstances but rather that his circumstances were his own creation. Evidently, all he had to do to change his life was to believe that it had changed. What a load of crap! He got up from his desk to discuss it with the First Censor. These books were falsifying facts. They claimed that a thing was not the thing itself, and that reality was the sum of our thoughts. But surely we have no thoughts. If we all turned to thinking, what would be left for the government to do?

Taking off his glasses, the First Censor rubbed his eyes, then rested his chin in his palm. Pointing his pudgy fingers at the rules, he pelted the new censor with questions. "Do these books call for revolutions or overthrowing the political, economic, or social system? Do they cast doubt on administrative decisions? Threaten the position of our local currency? Disturb the stock market? Do they harm the fabric of society?"

The new censor shook his head. "No, actually it's the opposite—they tell you that you must be happy and that the world is beautiful, even though it's—"

"Exactly," the First Censor interrupted. "These are *good* books. We must fill the bookstores with them. They were written in service of the System."

With a sigh, the new censor went back to his desk and noted that the book was approved. More goddamned books fit for circulation!

The First Censor's voice was cheerful. "See? You're getting the hang of it. You're asking all the right questions. Are you done for the day?"

Indeed, he had finished his work without banning a single book and was up to his ears in shame. Every time he heard one of the censors gleefully calling out that he'd found "twenty violations on a single page," he nearly died of envy. Why didn't they give *him* books like that? Books he could actually ban?

He handed in his reports to the First Censor, who approved them for submission to the Department Head.

"Aren't you going to read the books too?" he asked the First Censor.

"I've read them before. That was just another test."

"And have I passed?"

"They were easy books."

"Give me a challenging one, then."

"You're not ready." The First Censor handed him another batch.

"No more personal reflections," the new censor begged. "Please."

"A book censor must *not* enjoy what he reads."

"Am I supposed to spend six hours a day reading things I hate?"

The Second Censor answered from the desk over. "The more you hate the book, the better."

He hadn't yet grasped how dangerous it was. Why couldn't a person just read things that were entertaining, full of exciting profanity and transgressive thoughts, and write a report based on whatever offending lines they'd collected? What harm could there be in that? But the Second Censor had leaned forward, cupping his hand to his lips, and mouthed exaggeratedly, "*Because you don't want what happened to the Secretary to happen to you.*"

"What happened to the Secretary?"

"He fell in love with books and *lost his badge*," the other man whispered.

The new censor's eyebrows rose. "Really?"

Nodding, the Second Censor continued. "The Department Head didn't want to fire him, so they transferred him to administrative duties. Just last year, he was sitting right where you are now, but then he fell victim to the reading malady, could hardly tell the difference between books and the real world. He started muttering to himself, seeing things that we couldn't see, chasing the rabbits. Books drove him out of his mind! His reports were reviewed, and then he was brought in for questioning because he approved what should have been banned." He paused. "Do you know how he answered the investigators' questions?" Then he leaned in and hissed, "He lapsed into interpretation."

Clucking their tongues mechanically, the censors droned, "Alas, alas, what a terrible end. Interpretation is a censor's undoing. It's the last thing you should ever do."

Though he was afraid of the answer, the new censor asked, "And then what?"

"Because of his advanced age, the Department Head took pity on him. The case was shelved and, instead of imprisonment, he got a job as the department secretary. He had to sign a pledge at the Administrative Court, promising never to go back to reading. Would all that have happened to him, I wonder, if he hadn't enjoyed it? It is *essential* for us to hate what we read."

The Second Censor gestured toward a new batch of books on his desk. Just as he was about to reach for one, the Department Secretary walked into the office.

The censors' faces stiffened into mummy-like masks as they went back to the pages in front of them. Like statues, they sat. When a rabbit came into the room, no one attempted to shoo it away.

The Secretary was oddly cheerful for a former book censor tarred by scandal. "Good morning!" he chirped.

The new censor thought that if he had been branded a heretic and suspected of treason, he would never smile again for the rest of his life. The Secretary must be a lunatic—that or he was truly evil.

He was repulsed by the old man. He felt the muscles in his forearms begin to twitch; he couldn't for a moment forget that he was in the same room as a traitor. He peered at the man's face, hoping to find a sign of repentance. He wanted to forgive him for what he'd done; if only he had crept into the room with his head hung low, his face stained with regret, and no white rabbit trailing him. But real criminals are shameless. He found himself thinking of his own wife and daughter. How could this abominable old man have risked their safety by approving poisonous books? It was as bad as selling expired medicines or donkey meat! How he'd love to punch the imbecile in the face. Beady-eyed, he watched as the Secretary walked up to the First Censor's desk and gave him a new volume.

"Here's a book for inspection."

The First Censor looked at the title. "It's banned."

"This is a new edition, in a new translation."

"We've banned three editions of this book already."

"It's the law."

The First Censor grumbled. "They keep wasting our time with these games. A new translation, a new edition, a new publishing house—and every time we have to read the wretched thing again."

"I'll read it!"

The new censor wasn't sure what had pushed him to volunteer for the task. At the time, all he'd wanted to do was ban something to annoy the old traitor, to get on his nerves. He had spent the past few days reluctantly signing off on drivel. Now he wanted to see how it felt to censor dangerous material, to protect society from real and present harm. He walked over and snatched the book, then went back to his desk feeling pleased with himself. Finally, he'd gotten his hands on something worth his time, and he would be credited with banning it forever!

The Secretary smiled cryptically. Gaunt and gray-haired, wrinkles overwhelmed his skin, spreading weblike from the corners of his mouth. He wore round gold-framed spectacles—a living, breathing relic.

The First Censor shook his head. "You're not ready."

"How much time do I have to submit the report?"

"You can't read that book."

"How much time?"

The First Censor sighed, then took a calculator from the drawer. "How many pages? Three hundred and ninety-six—if you read a hundred and twenty pages a day, you'll be done with the report in three and a half. But I'll give you five days to finish it."

"Agreed!" the new censor cried at once.

The Secretary laughed. As he left the room, followed by the white rabbit, he muttered, "Good luck reading *Zorba the Greek* in five days!"

5

"IN MY ROOM, a wardrobe sits.

And inside that, Wolf lurks and wails.

Inside Wolf, my grandma knits

A bellyful of fairy tales."

The child had been saying this since yesterday.

Pulling him by the hand into her room, she opened the wooden wardrobe and pointed to the empty space inside. "Can you see it, Baba? Can you see it?"

When his wife saw how serious their daughter's condition had become, her eyes welled. But he just ground his teeth and whispered, "Don't get upset over nothing." He ruffled the little girl's hair and a smattering of baby powder stuck to his palm. "It's time for school," he said. "Shall we go?"

All color drained from her face and her mouth curved down. She dove into the wardrobe and shut herself in, alone with a wolf that had eaten a grandmother. School scared her more than the wolf did.

When his wife tried to force her from the wardrobe, the child lashed out in what had become an almost daily episode of sobbing and kicking. She refused to leave her room because she wanted to play with the "wolf in the wardrobe," and she sneaked lumps of sugar from the kitchen for the winged unicorn in case it showed up too. His wife was worried. The little one didn't seem interested in playing with other children. She would speak to stuffed animals, trees, ants, fairies, spiders, bedbugs, stray cats, goldfinches, wolves. Any kind of creature—real or imaginary—as long as it wasn't a human being.

"Isn't it obvious?" his wife whispered.

"What is?"

"Our daughter . . . she's . . . " She lowered her voice even more. "She's imagining things!"

He held his expression steady. He could not appear to be losing control. "It's just a passing thing, like the flu."

"She's getting worse."

"It'll go away by itself."

Hugging the girl close, he covered her eyes with his palm the way he did every time she had a panic attack. The screaming stopped and she calmed down, but then her muffled crying began. He could feel how fragile and skinny she was, like a toothpick—one snap and she would break in his arms. Her frailness terrified him, as did those small eyes and the slender neck that nearly fit between his thumb and forefinger. How would a child like her survive in the real world?

His daughter hated school but loved almost every other place: the beach, the park, their home. She felt most comfortable in her wooden wardrobe, with its white paint and carved designs.

Just a couple days ago, she had decided the wardrobe needed to be pink and started painting it with her mother's nail polish. It ran out after barely covering two inches of surface. Frustrated, her face flushed and her breath grew ragged: an endless stream of pink nail polish was meant to flow out of the little bottle. It was a magic bottle, after all. The pink stain on the wardrobe vexed his wife, but nobody did anything about it. When this happened, he had been busy reading *Zorba*.

"She's not like the other children," his wife said to him once, at the park. She'd let go of their daughter's hand, allowing her to run over to a flock of pigeons that had settled on the pavement near some scattered rice. When the pigeons fluttered away, the child stamped her feet and burst into tears. She had panic attacks at odd times. He knew now, for instance, that they could be brought on by a full moon, or when she saw a skyscraper or a mosaic mural of the President. Of course, no one could ever know that images of the President rattled her, especially the large ones—something like that could land them in hot water. It was only by accident that he discovered putting his palm over her eyes did the trick, reminding him of the goldfinch his father had bought him on Purification Day. He remembered his father's warning that they must cover the cage with a black cloth: otherwise, the bird would panic and knock itself dead against the bars.

Why had the dead bird flashed before his eyes? At the time, his daughter had been banging her head against the wall, screaming that she didn't want to go to school. Gently drawing close to her, he'd rested his palm across her eyes. In a few minutes, she had stopped crying.

"How did you do that?" his wife had asked.

He'd shrugged. Even he didn't know.

The child worried him. She showed disturbing symptoms, and practically everything she said was nonsense. One time he asked her what she wished for most in the world. There were only two things she wanted: for animals not to be afraid of her, and to fly higher than their house, higher than she'd ever managed to with fairy dust—which was really just baby powder. He thought he should do something before her imagination spun out of control, but reassured himself that, as soon as she started elementary school, reality would set in. Schools were designed to snuff out imagination. At least, he supposed they were.

The trip to the park had ended abruptly when his daughter grew disturbed because the pigeons had flown away. With his palm over her eyes, he held her close to his chest and walked home calmly.

Yesterday morning, the child said she had been up all night, soaring in the sky with a fairy no bigger than a thumb. His wife was fed up with her stories; nobody could understand where they were coming from. When his wife tried to pull her off the bed, she burst into tears and flapped her arms furiously, threatening to fly away and never come back. She

37

charged at the dressing table, picked up the baby powder, and shook some on her head, saying she'd fly out the window like all the other children who never grow up, and she would never have to set foot in school again.

In the end, she went to kindergarten, her hair whitened with fairy dust and her eyes red from crying. Only when her mother let her wear her sparkly ruby shoes instead of her usual black ones did she agree to go. The ruby shoes supposedly meant something in some story. He had bought them—along with a dozen ruffled skirts and poorly sewn princess costumes—on Purification Day last year, from one of the kiosks that sold Old World souvenirs.

He had to take his daughter to school himself. His wife was lying on the living room couch, moaning in pain. Was it her head? Her neck? Her broken heart? A scarf was wrapped around her neck and her skin reeked of muscle rub. She had tied a white cloth around her head as well. It was like this every morning now. Punishing him for letting those books into their bed. For letting them take up her spot and bite her. And in spite of all the pleasant surprises of the past few days—since he'd started reading *Zorba*—she resented him. Even when he pulled her from the kitchen or the laundry room so they could make love, she would still feel jealous, especially after hearing him murmur the names of other women in his sleep.

"Who's this Anna Karenina? Is there someone else?" she'd ask. And for a moment, he wondered if there was.

"You take her today. I haven't slept—I can't sleep properly in her bed, it's too small." He nodded, muttering his agreement as he opened the cereal box and poured some into a little bowl. His daughter told him that her bowl was smaller than all of the three bears' bowls, and he wondered what on earth she was blathering about. He glanced at his wife. She had crooked her arm over the sleep mask covering her eyes. He hadn't slept well either, but he didn't dare say it.

6

THE SECRETARY had been right.

You can't read Zorba the Greek *in five days. And however long it takes you, you'll never be the same again.*

Maybe it's not something everyone should read, the new censor thought. Perhaps one must deserve a book before they have the right to read it. *Why am I thinking like this? Am I losing my faith in the System?* He underlined a sentence in pencil and made a note of the violation. Mustering his courage, he plodded on. One line at a time, he would protect the surface of the world from meaning.

He had found more than enough violations to ban the book: phrases that offended, transgressed, blasphemed. Practically every taboo had been broached, but for some strange reason, the thought of people not reading *Zorba* made his stomach ache.

The Secretary again popped into his mind—the former book censor who had fallen in love with books and stumbled into the dark abyss of interpretation. *Why risk losing so much, and for what? You've got a house, a wife, a child. Is this what you want for your daughter? For her father to be entangled in meaning?* He left the department, walked to the window at the end of the marble corridor, and looked out at the garden next door. What was the point of having a garden here? It was a breeding ground for rabbits. He spotted a white rabbit, and it saw him too: it stopped chewing grass, stood upright, and fixed him with a pointed look. Why did he always feel like there was a rabbit waiting just around the corner? He backed away from the window and returned to the office. He *wouldn't* betray the System. He *wouldn't* lose his faith. And no matter what, he *wouldn't* be made the Secretary's secretary by an act of charity from the Department Head. He *had* to protect others from reading this despicable book. A debauched man who crept into women's beds for duty's sake? A man who condemned marriage and had no faith in God nor fear of the devil, who renounced his country and doubted every kind of established order? Damn *Zorba*!

A white rabbit burst into the department, hopped over to his desk, and rose to its hind legs. Its whiskers and nose twitched. The fur on its long ears and those red glassy eyes made him feel dizzy. Never in his life had he liked rabbits, even as a small boy. He spat out an expletive. The censors chuckled, and he felt his fingernails biting into his palms. He flung an eraser at the creature, but it had already retreated. It sniffed for a while at the rubber weapon, which had fallen at its feet, then rose again on its hind legs. The new censor tried to kick it, but it escaped, springing nimbly out the door. Just then, a fantasy crossed his mind: if he managed to kill even a single rabbit, all of them would disappear and he'd have rabbit broth for dinner.

He leapt after it. The rabbit quickened its pace. He began to run, swearing. "Get over here! Now!" It made a right turn into one of the offices. Where could it have gone? The new censor froze as he arrived at the Secretary's desk. The old man was down on one knee, holding out a lettuce leaf. The damned rabbit was eating out of his hand.

That traitor, that booklover, that former censor who had fallen into the crime of interpretation, was feeding the rabbit!

"What do you want?"

"I—"

He couldn't bring himself to finish his sentence. *I want that rabbit.* A rush of shame washed over him. "Don't feed the rabbits!" he said instead. "The department is crawling with them, and they crap in the corridors."

"You can't stop the rabbits."

"Ridiculous! Of course I can."

"They always turn up. That's what they do."

He was suddenly taken aback. Why was it so easy to talk to this old man? "Wait, do I know you?"

The Secretary shrugged. "How should I know?"

Why did he feel so familiar? "How old are you?"

"What a question." The Secretary patted the rabbit's head and stood up. "Have you read *Zorba* yet?"

"How could I not have?"

"I haven't received your report."

"I was just about to finish it when this *thing* showed up."

As he spoke, the rabbit bounced out of the office, munching on the scrap of lettuce in its mouth. It seemed unusually happy for an animal, as if it had accomplished what it meant to do. The Secretary sat on top of his desk, took off his glasses, and rubbed his eyes. The new censor stared at the wealth of wrinkles on his face.

"And what did you find?" the old man asked.

"What do you mean?"

"In *Zorba*."

"Oh, transgressions against God, offending public morals, threatening public order—everything!"

Laughing, the Secretary's left eyebrow arched. "And did you like it?"

The censor's heart skipped a beat. "What a question!" he said, his lips twitching.

Turning on his heel, he strode out of the office. He would not speak to that snake anymore. The old man would drag him into the gutter of readers and, before he knew it, he'd wake up one day and find himself drowning in interpretation—whatever that meant!

ADMINISTRATIVE DECISION /1.3/ OF THE SECOND
YEAR AFTER THE REVOLUTION

THE BOOK CENSOR'S MANUAL FOR CORRECT READING

1/ A thing is what it is, a word means itself, and
every word has only one meaning, which is the
meaning approved by the Censorship Authority.

2/ A censor must consider words and formations
in pure isolation, avoiding all ideas and
interpretations.

3/ A book censor should look out for three words:
God, Government, and Sex. These words and their
neighboring words should be inspected.

4/ A book censor is not allowed to spend time on
a book past the deadline provided by the First
Censor unless he files for an exception.

5/ A book censor must ban all books that address
forbidden subjects such as philosophy,
semiotics, linguistics, hermeneutics, sociology,
politics, and other such useless subjects.

6/ Books about astrology and zodiac signs must
be banned, as well as books of sorcery and
magic and books that contain information that
is harmful to the public, such as how to
manufacture hashish, intoxicants, and other
substances of a similar nature.

44

7/ Books that incite violence must be banned, even
   if no crime has been committed.

8/ Academic books that circulate research where the
   results do not match those of research conducted
   by government labs must be banned.

9/ Books that contradict sound logic or lie about
   reality must be banned, such as books where
   animals talk or carpets fly, as well as books
   that spread superstition.

10/ Poetry collections, novels, and all other
    works of literature that do not adhere to the
    principles of the Popular Movement for Positive
    Realism must be banned.

SECTION 1: PROHIBITIONS PERTAINING TO GOD

* It is forbidden to circulate sacred books
  amongst the public, except in their simplified
  editions which have been approved by the
  Religious Law Oversight Committee.

* Religious books must be referred to the
  Religious Law Oversight Committee to verify
  their conformance to the True Faith as certified
  by the Supreme Authority for Religious Law,
  following the issuance of Administrative
  Decision 10.5 concerning religious reform.

* Books must be banned that, in a religious

context, use terms such as <u>angel</u>, <u>djinn</u>, <u>ifrit</u>, <u>devil</u>, etc.

* Books that use religious terms in literary contexts must be referred to the Religious Law Oversight Committee to be approved for circulation.
* Books must be banned that address the unknowable: heaven, hell, the day of judgment, reincarnation, karma, the soul, etc.

SECTION 2: PROHIBITIONS PERTAINING TO THE GOVERNMENT

* Books must be banned that undermine public order and attack political figures, the Party, the government, or the President. Books that cast doubts on the country's political and adminis-trative system, or threaten the local currency or the economic situation, must also be banned.
* Books that address public affairs, political issues, or the presidential person, in a manner consistent with the interests of the System, must, before being approved, be referred to the Party Headquarters to confirm that they are fit for circulation.
* A book censor must ban any book that contains words such as: democracy, parliament, internet,

information revolution, Twitter/X, Instagram, Facebook, smart application, computer, peaceful transfer of power, ballot box, voting, polling, sit-in, demonstrations, march, peaceful resistance, political reform, coup, power, the military, corruption, embezzlements, and other such terms belonging to the Old World.

* History books that address the Old World and time periods from before the Revolution must be banned.
* Books that cover the history of the Popular Movement for Positive Realism must be banned, except for those that are issued by the Censorship Authority.

SECTION 3: PROHIBITIONS PERTAINING TO SEX

* Books must be banned that use words which arouse and encourage indecent behavior, or that use, in an improper manner, words that offend public modesty such as <u>kiss</u>, <u>breast</u>, <u>thigh</u>, and other body parts.
* Books must be banned which speak of young boys, queerness, or illicit relationships. Books must also be banned that address sexual relationships except in the form approved by the government, which is within the bounds of a marriage between a male and a female.

7

HE HAD TO CONFESS—at least to himself—that since *Zorba*, many things in his life had changed. Things he didn't dare mention to anyone, because the last thing a book censor should do is admit his enemy's virtues. They were probably just tricks, which the enemy used to tempt him. But why did bread suddenly taste as though he'd never had bread before? And why was the air so sweet and pure? Like butterflies shedding cocoons, the extraordinary emerged from hiding. The surface of his humble world was pulled back, exposing tenderness beneath.

The day he read *I should fill my soul with flesh*, he grabbed his wife from the kitchen and carried her to their bed. He ran his hand over every inch of her body as if rediscovering it. But he wasn't rediscovering the world, he was creating it. Was this how the first human felt when he was introduced to that magnificent sponge they called language?

He knew that Zorba was a debauched animal, but he didn't understand how he could love that animal. When he reminded himself of the man's unforgivable sins, sometimes he managed to hate him. But he would always return to Zorba, broken, because in spite of everything, Zorba was both a scoundrel and a nobleman. Zorba was playing tag with him, and he refused to be caught. Every time he stuck a label on the man, Zorba would come back and prove it wrong, and every time he put him on a shelf, Zorba pulled a fast one and jumped off altogether. He thought this was another act of sabotage from the enemy, but how could he give his final verdict on Zorba when the man was constantly transforming?

The lines stuck like birdlime to his memory. He was able to recall entire paragraphs, as if he'd been reading the book all his life. Before *Zorba*, the trees in the street had been anonymous, but now he called them by names he'd read in the book: *A tamarisk, a wild fig tree, a tuft of reeds, some bitter mullein.* The world was recreating itself before his eyes, as if the big bang had just happened and *he* had been appointed the grantor of titles. Except, of course, he knew that the government had finished that job a long time ago. He knew that he was caught in the throat of a word that would never utter him, a word that he, too, would never let past his lips.

Over the past few days, he had begun to show unmistakable symptoms of the disease. He found himself attracted to certain books, and would sneak them out of the bags and boxes that lined the corridors at work, scurrying out to his car with them tucked inside his coat. These were books he felt *he* was meant to read, books that wanted him in particular, that called his name. What if they had been assigned to another censor? Never! The books had chosen *him*. They had filled up his wardrobe and his bed and thrown out his wife. Everything he'd been warned of about books had come true: he'd become someone else.

When he read that Zorba had *cracked life's shell* and gone *straight to its very substance*, it occurred to him that he was missing a lot by staying on the surface. Worst of all were the lines that spoke of what lay below: *When will people's ears open, boss? When shall we have our eyes open to see?* But he was unsure of what he saw. Underneath the thin shell of erring language—guilty of indecency, blasphemy, inciting coups, and more—there was a delicate, strange world he was dying to touch.

He knew the book was poisonous, and that it was his duty to keep society sterile, free from intruding thoughts. It was exactly as he had read, *perfectly clear distilled water without any bacteria, but also without life*. But what was he supposed to do? Approve a book that was full of bacteria and nourishment, or let the human race die of starvation?

But who would notice the absence of a book like that? People who don't eat don't get hungry. His job was to fill the bookstores with drivel. He had to make sure no one craved books. He'd come to understand that they weren't waging a war against books so much as a war against reading. Reading was a bad habit, but you couldn't keep people from doing it, just as you couldn't keep them from smoking or having sex.

All you could do was limit their options, give them the illusion of choice. Then, all on their own, they would turn away. In the future, he and the other censors wouldn't *need* to ban any books—no one would read them anyway. It was as if he could see the future of humankind in a crystal ball.

Yes, he had to ban the book. How could he ever put this into society's hands? A book that mocked everything he'd vowed to protect. What if someone read it and began to spout blasphemy, or opposed the government and went around saying, as Zorba did, *I am not a patriot, and will not be, whatever it costs me!* If an idea like that gained traction, what would become of the state's institutions: the army, the police, the special guard, or the media? What if demonstrators filled the squares and there was a revolution against the Revolution, and more people died in the streets? What if every man who read this book believed what Zorba said about it being a sin—an unforgivable sin—to let a woman sleep alone, and left the world swarming with bastards?

Even so, there was one thing about the book that confused him, a single line which, to him, seemed reason enough to forgive Zorba's sins. *I spit on those books of yours. Not everything that exists can be found in your books.* How could he ban one book that spit on the rest? Those rectangular beasts that had kicked him out of his familiar world and into a place where a thing was no longer itself. He was so tired. A vague feeling that nobody understood him took hold: not his wife, not his child, not the other censors. Only Zorba understood him—he alone knew what books could do. He felt he owed Zorba that much at least. They were agreed that books were wretched, even though they could only meet on the pages of one. This book was wicked, but at least it was a book that damned itself.

He had finished his report, jotting down his comments up to the last offending line. Sometimes, the sheer horror of what he was reading made him feel the sky was about to fall squarely on his head. But once he was done, he sat lost in thought, staring at the task schedule on the wall before him. Soon, the First Censor would erase *Zorba*'s name from the "books under inspection" column. It was like parting with a piece of his soul. His heart was heavy. He was a man at port waving farewell to a friend sailing to the other side of the world. Would he be able to sneak another look at those pages every now and then? Would he be able to see the island and smell the sea?

Picking up the pen again, he added one last line to his report:

Despite its many offending lines, this book actually belittles and discredits every book. I, therefore, believe that it serves the interests of the System and accordingly recommend approving the book, in pursuance of public interest.

8

THE HOUSES were all the same: white cubes with small, tightly spaced windows. The streets were narrow, and at this early hour they were choked with tiny gray cars driven by people just like him, dressed in khaki pants and beige shirts.

In everyone he saw, there was an uncanny reflection of himself. Even so, he felt inexplicably lonely, as if none of these teeming clones bore him any true resemblance. Was he still standing on the surface of the world, brandishing his spear, eager to hurl it at the white rabbit? Or was he—deep down—utterly exhausted, wanting no more than to sit for a while and mourn the absence of Zorba? He was so tired that he didn't even stop his daughter from having a conversation with an imaginary stray cat. She claimed she had seen the cat crossing the road at a red light, and that it was off to buy a pair of shoes.

As a good father does, he usually did his duty to bring the child back to reality, back to—as the First Censor would say—**WHAT COULD BE PROVEN IN A LAB**. It was rumored that each new baby was born with certain vestiges of the Old

World: things cemented in human memory for thousands of years, tracing back to bygone civilizations, such as fables and fairy tales. The Guidance and Counseling Authority allocated a huge budget each year for awareness-raising campaigns: **DOES YOUR CHILD SUFFER FROM IMAGINATION? DON'T HESITATE TO ASK FOR HELP! DON'T LET THEM SUFFER! YOU'RE NOT ALONE!** They were messages he knew well, even believed in. And he was aware that his daughter seemed to be falling behind compared to her peers. But today he was simply tired. The last time he had taken his daughter to the clinic to be vaccinated, there was a flyer about incontinence and another with a picture of a terrified child around the age of four, alone in a bedroom with enormous monsters of his own making that were trying to devour him. **SWOLLEN IMAGINATIONS CAN BE CURED!** the tagline said, with a hotline provided. One of the flyers listed the symptoms that parents could use to tell whether or not their child was afflicted: nightmares or vivid dreams, imaginary friends, stories from unknown sources . . . He hadn't needed to read on.

Arriving at his daughter's school, he felt he was seeing it for the first time, even though it was just as he had always known it: a square building that looked like every other building in the city. Nurseries and kindergartens were permitted to paint their walls pale yellow, but, when it came to elementary school, things were different. The walls were khaki, and the students learned the Principles of Positive Realism, the world in its prescribed logical form:

54

HUMAN EXISTENCE IS SUFFERING.
THE ROOT OF SUFFERING IS DESIRE.
THE ROOT OF DESIRE IS IMAGINATION.

Three simple principles that, to him, had always seemed to explain everything. The Founding Fathers had discovered—after the fall of democracies, the rationing of technology, the revolution against the information revolution, and an in-depth study of their history—that the only way to create a happy city was to empty its inhabitants of their desires, except those desires that are essential for the survival of the species. They had decided that imagination was the origin of all past evils: every drop of spilled blood, every strike, every instrument of torture, every useless human invention, every pornographic film, every mental and nervous disease, every failed marital relationship. Every miserable idea that a person might pursue at some point or another was an undesirable secretion of their imagination.

From then on, the System's aim was to create a human being who, after a long day's work, wanted nothing else but to go home. This was the epitome of human perfection—something he had failed to achieve on a personal level. He went home every night drenched with the desire to read. How was a weak-willed addict like him supposed to be any good at raising a kid?

The new censor peered at his daughter. She looked like a primitive creature, unable to cope. As soon as she caught sight of her school, she curled up in the back seat and wept.

When she began to kick and scream, he covered her eyes with his palm, scooped her up, and delivered her to the teacher standing at the entrance. She was still thrashing and calling out to him when he left—"Baba! Help me!"—as if she stood at the entrance to hell. Of course, he knew as well as anyone else that hell did not exist.

9

"THE BOSS asked for you," the First Censor said through pursed lips.

The new censor had just walked into the department. He hadn't even sat down. Judging by his supervisor's disapproving tone, he knew it must be something to do with the recommendation he'd attached to his report.

The phone rang. "Yes, he's just arrived—of course," the First Censor said, nodding toward the Department Head's office.

The other censors shook their heads in pity, as if he'd been sentenced to death. He felt as though he were headed for the guillotine on a tumbrel pulled by sickly horses, packed shoulder to shoulder with others doomed to exile from the surface of the world. Their eyes tracked him, and he dropped a pen on the floor to watch the heads of the seven censors bob down as he bent to pick it up. Then the First Censor cleared his throat and they all went back to digging for violations. On their desks, each censor held a book open as if it were a rabbit, pinned spread-eagle to a board, its belly split wide for dissection.

He left the department with rabbits on his mind, spied a turd on the marble tiles of the corridor leading to the Secretary's office, and then found himself standing before the old man.

As soon as he saw him, the Secretary jumped up. "What have you done? Are you out of your mind?" he whispered.

For a moment, the new censor didn't know what to say. His throat had gone dry—it seemed his newborn career was about to draw its last breath. "Is it really that bad?"

Removing his spectacles, the old man wiped the lenses with a corner of his shirt. "I don't know," he said, then looked up at him, the shadow of a smile on his lips. "You can't approve a book that's been banned three times already. Next time, if you want to approve a book—"

Before he could finish his sentence, the door of the Department Head's office opened. The Secretary coughed, his face suddenly red. The Department Head stood at the door, examining the new censor. He was about forty-five years old with piercing dark eyes, a thick black mustache, and tanned skin—a ruggedly handsome man. Something about his face made the new censor swallow hard and loud. *It's the eyes*, he thought. *Definitely the eyes.*

"Are you the new censor?"

"Yes."

The Department Head nodded for him to come in. He wasn't sure why, but he had to fight the urge to offer a military salute. Perhaps it was the khaki jacket that emphasized his wide shoulders and thick, muscled arms.

Once inside, the new censor stood transfixed at the sight of wall-to-wall bookshelves. He held his breath, wanting to gasp but not daring to. The shelves were solid wood with a rolling ladder. Book, after book, after book.

"What do you think?"

"It's massive." He kept his answer brief. How could he gush over the beauty of a library in the Book Censorship Authority? His loyalty would be called into question.

The Department Head rapped his fingers on the spines. "After thirty years of book censorship, this library is my most important achievement!"

"You've read them all?"

"Read, and banned them too."

The new censor's jaw dropped. "*All* of these books are banned?"

The Department Head narrowed his eyes. "They don't count as books anymore since they're not being read. I like to think of them as trophies."

No different than deer heads hanging on a hunter's walls. This wasn't a library—it was a cemetery, kept there for show. It made his skin crawl.

The Department Head opened a drawer and took out a stack of documents, one of which the new censor recognized as his report. "Your work is meticulous, that's good," his superior said. "You haven't missed a single line."

The new censor felt his confidence returning. For the first time since that morning, he could breathe comfortably.

"Thank you for the effort you've clearly put into this," his boss continued.

"I was just doing my duty . . . "

"I think you have a real future here."

He couldn't believe it. A real future? What did that mean? A promotion? Becoming a lead censor, or—who knows—maybe even a bookstore inspector? A higher salary and a bigger electricity quota so he could read at night . . . He was lost in the daydream when he heard, "Are you happy here?"

"Er, yes, yes." He rubbed the back of his neck.

"Is something wrong?"

"Well, it's the rabbits."

The Department Head's mouth stretched into what ought to have been a smile, but instead a tight-lipped grimace creased his face. He looked deep into the new censor's eyes. "The rabbits are a side effect of the job."

The new censor nodded, his shoulders slumping a little.

"As for the recommendation . . . "

"Yes?"

"You recommended that the book be approved."

"I did."

"You were thinking of the interests of the System. I understand that, but—"

Hanging his head, the new censor let out a sigh. "I shouldn't have been thinking at all."

"Exactly. A book censor should *never* wade into interpretation."

"Yes."

"And you—you're swimming in it."

Heat flushed up the new censor's neck and his palms began to sweat. He wished he could wipe himself off the surface of the world right then and there. Faced with the Department Head's words and that look on his face—the one that mocked him for his failure not as a censor but as a reader—he felt the smallest he'd ever been.

He had never heard of the crime of "interpretation" until he became a book censor. Even then, he hadn't understood what it involved. When he'd asked the First Censor, his answer was that interpretation was an Old-World practice from the time when readers thought they could engage with texts to create meaning. "But," the First Censor had continued, "*we* don't have to deal with such issues. The only meaning in our lives comes to us from the government. Our duty as book censors is to block all avenues of interpretation."

The Department Head's voice interrupted his thoughts. "Interpretation is the responsibility of the authorities."

"Understood." He blurted out his answer, even though what he'd heard had surprised him. It made perfect sense, even though he'd never thought of it that way before. He used to think that interpretation was a crime, but now he'd discovered it was a matter of responsibility, a task to be taken on by a higher power—but definitely not by him, the naive reader.

10

FOR THE REST OF THE DAY, he sat stiff and unable to read. He tried to look through the books on his desk but found nothing of interest. Why didn't they give him another novel? After all, everyone knew he'd written an excellent report—apart from the final recommendation.

What had the Department Head said? *You're swimming in interpretation.*

The man had been laughing at him, implying that even if he'd *wanted* to commit a crime, he shouldn't have made such a production of it. He felt ridiculous. What an idiot he'd been to have tried to express his opinion as an impersonal one—he would have been better off simply writing, "Yes, Zorba is a filthy bastard, but I love him and I don't want the book to be banned!" Resting his head on the desk, he reflected on his meeting with the Department Head, thinking about the enormous bookcase made of dark wood, that cemetery of forbidden books. *If the Department Head gets to keep his victims' corpses, why can't I have my copy of* Zorba? He missed it dreadfully, as if he'd lost a friend. Roaring waves, rustling grass, the calls of the old woman who owned the hotel—he could hear them all. The old woman had a beauty spot on her chin from which sprang hair, like . . . Like what? Like sow bristles! He had chuckled at the image conjured up by those words. Later, he'd pretended not to like it—it was bad manners to make fun of a lady's beauty spots. But where was Zorba?

He closed his eyes and soon found himself on the island, sitting cross-legged in front of a man who looked like Sinbad the Sailor. *You're a good fellow*, the man said. *You lack nothing . . . Except just one thing—folly!* The man punched him on the shoulder and he woke in a panic.

He lifted his head and saw the censors laughing—a thin line of drool trailed from the side of his mouth to the top of his desk. How long had he been asleep? From the heat in his cheeks and the ice-pick pain at the back of his neck, it felt like he'd spent a whole night there. He looked at the First Censor, who smirked and said, "Good morning!"

"I lost track of . . . I . . ."

"What did the boss say?"

He realized they were desperate to know what had happened. Clearing his throat, he puffed up his chest. "He said it was an excellent report."

The censors stared at him—it clearly wasn't what they'd expected to hear.

Lacing his fingers behind his head, he leaned back and

cracked his knuckles. "He said I have a real future here," he added, smiling wider.

"The boss said that?"

"Yes."

"G-g-good," stammered the First Censor, and the seven censors flashed him seven perfectly synchronized smiles. Before the conversation could go on any longer, he got up and crossed the narrow corridor that led to the Secretary's office. The stench of rabbit droppings followed him all the way. He had something to say to this strange old man constantly shadowed by rabbits.

When he arrived at the doorway to the office, he caught the Secretary fumbling with something under his desk. His wrinkled face had turned red again. He recognized the sound—he could never mistake it. The soft thump of a closing book.

He was pleased: the old man was at his mercy. After all, he'd signed a pledge never to read again, and here he was, reading in secret. Damn him, the rotten traitor!

"What are you reading?" he asked, springing the question on him.

"Nothing."

"Where's the boss?"

"He left."

"You were reading on the sly."

Instead of getting flustered, the old man gave him a sideways look. "And?"

Why doesn't he look scared? "Maybe I'll tell the boss."

"Doubtful."

"What's there to stop me?"

"A reader never betrays another reader."

The new censor's face flushed. "What are you saying? What kind of bullshit is that?"

The Secretary winked at him. "We readers understand each other."

He wanted to say, *I'm not a reader*, meaning, *I'm not a traitor*, but his tongue refused to cooperate. "You're demented," he muttered.

"What do you want now?"

"I want the book."

"What book?"

"*Zorba the Greek*. I want the copy I inspected."

The old man raised his gray eyebrows. "Why?"

"I want to keep it. I'm the one who inspected it and I have a right to—"

Shaking his head, the old man said, "You don't have the right to anything. It belongs to the government."

"But the Department Head . . . his library . . . all those books—"

"Yes, it's a wonderful library."

He didn't even try to hide his envy. "I want my own private library too."

"That's not possible."

"If you don't give me back my book, I'll tell everyone your little secret. You'll be fired, or worse, I suppose."

The Secretary looked at him with narrowed eyes. "You wouldn't dare."

The censor held his stare. When the old man realized he wasn't backing down, he let out a heavy sigh, took off his spectacles, and rubbed his eyes. "Go back to your office. I'll see what I can do."

"Not before I know—"

"Know what?"

"What you were reading."

The old man slapped his thigh and took the book out of hiding.

TO WONDERLAND

1

EITHER THE DREAM was very deep, or the Book Censor fell very slowly, for he had plenty of time as he went down to look about him and wonder what would happen next. He looked at the sides of the dream and noticed they were lined with bookshelves. Down, down, down. Would the fall never come to an end? He thought he must be getting somewhere near the center of the earth, that he would soon fall right through to the other side, where Zorba had gone. Then: Bang! He crashed onto a pile of books.

Awakened, the Book Censor mulled over what Alice had been thinking. He wondered if it had been her own thought, or if she had stolen it from him. Or had she somehow crept into his head and stolen his voice, so the two of them were now one and the same? He wondered what he would find on the other side of the world. *People that walked with their heads downward,* and everything topsy-turvy? The System would never tolerate *that.*

Unlike *Zorba,* which he'd read as a censor, the ruling on *Alice in Wonderland* had been issued many years ago—banned in all translations and editions—which meant that he had *deliberately* read a banned book. His first crime! It was a petty crime of no consequence, he decided. A white lie. Instead of dwelling on his guilt, he couldn't help but wonder: Had he read the best translation? He thought it was excellent, but who was he to judge? He'd only taken his first steps as a reader one book ago, and here he was thinking like a traitor!

And what about those other books he wasn't supposed to read? How could he miss out on those? If only he'd been there for the inaugural mass inspection, back when the new government was reassessing everything. The first-generation book censors had to read all the books that had ever been written so they could decide their fate. What an eventful year it must have been.

It was so unfair! When they had given him the mission of guarding the surface of the world, he'd never imagined he'd have to spend his time waiting on the shore while others, luckier than him, rode the waves to their heart's content. All he really wanted was to cross the sea and go back to that island, but Wonderland wouldn't leave him alone. It kept sending him rabbits. He used to hate such vermin. Now he wasn't sure how he felt about them.

What had gotten into him that day? Why had he snatched the book from the Secretary's hand, holding it hostage? "I'm keeping this till you give me *Zorba*!" he'd threatened, turning to leave. He hadn't understood why the old man held his fist to his lips.

"Listen, that book is from the boss's library. If he notices it's gone, he'll—"

"Then you'd better hurry and hand *Zorba* over."

He'd expected the Secretary to tease him, to say something like, *What's gotten into you? Don't tell me you've fallen in love with books!* But the old man had acted as if his desire to keep the novel was the most natural thing in the world.

"I'll try," he'd said.

Since then, a week had gone by and nothing had happened. *Zorba* hadn't been returned to him, and the Department Head hadn't noticed that *Alice in Wonderland* was missing. But at least the new censor now knew where the rabbits came from.

For the entire week, before his long fall to the center of the earth, the Secretary had shown up in his dreams saying the same thing every time: "Follow the white rabbit!" But he'd never warmed to the dubious man who kept smiling, carefree. *Delusional*, the new censor thought. And of course he didn't mind his new role as secretary, because any time the Department Head left his office, that traitor would creep into his library and sneak out with a book. He must have read those books dozens of times, right under the noses of the Administrative Judiciary Board, the Authority officials, and the Department Head himself. What the Department Head thought was a cemetery for books had turned out to be a living, breathing library! He didn't want to, but he found this a comforting thought.

And ever since that day—the day he'd arrived in Wonderland—the new book censor had more or less made peace with his indiscretions. Some books he read in secret, others in public. Sitting in his office, he wrote reports on the books that were assigned to him. But as soon as he finished his duties, he would sneak into the storeroom. And there—surrounded by dusty bags and boxes full of administrative reports, time cards, inventory logs, and the department's entire stockpile of correspondence—he read. If one of the other censors or administrators walked in on him, he could easily explain why he was there: He'd come to look for the "time-off request form." As for the book in his hand, he'd happened to pick it up out of one of the boxes and was simply leafing through it. No big deal.

"You must fully understand the nature of your job. These items you're inspecting are more dangerous than drugs or weapons—even love. They're books!" The First Censor's voice rang out in his head every time he picked up a new volume, quickening his pulse. He relished the madness that took hold of his body. A rush of blood flowed hot in his veins. He began to replay the First Censor's words over and over.

Alice in Wonderland was driving him mad. There wasn't a single offending line in the book, and yet it allowed the imagination to run wild. How had the Authority managed to ban it? Weren't they supposed to consider words and formations in pure isolation and avoid all ideas and interpretation? Something did not smell right. He recognized it at once, the stench of interpretation—it was forbidden to new censors, yet seemed to be permitted for senior ones. Who else could the Department Head have been referring to when he said that interpretation was the responsibility of those in charge?

Quizzing the First Censor about this had earned him an explanation. A special, five-person committee ruled on such books—spotless on the surface, insides riddled with worms. Finally, here was an admission that there was something deeper! His suspicions had been right all along: language wasn't merely a surface, and its tiny holes were full of wondrous scuttling creatures. He'd seen them with his own eyes. The First Censor's words—that at times we *must* resort to interpretation—were oddly consoling. In fact, the First Censor even had an additional manual: *The Interpretation Manual*! He'd asked to see a copy but was quickly reminded that he wasn't authorized. In ten years' time, at best, he'd be allowed to read it when—and if—he was promoted.

Frustrated, he'd gotten up from his desk and gone straight to the Secretary's office. Looking steadily into the old man's eyes, he whispered, "Give me *The Interpretation Manual*." The old man made no objection. Taking the manual out of a drawer, he calmly pushed it across the top of the desk, even getting up to close the door so the new censor could read it without getting caught. He didn't have to read much before he found exactly what he'd expected:

IF THE FIRST CENSOR IS FORCED TO RESORT TO
INTERPRETATION, AND WHERE THERE ARE SEVERAL
INTERPRETATIONS, HE MUST INVOKE THE PRIN-
CIPLE OF "PREVENTION IS BETTER THAN CURE,"
AND CHOOSE THE INTERPRETATION WHICH IS IN
THE BEST INTEREST OF THE SYSTEM, WHETHER
BY BANNING OR APPROVING THE BOOK.

"Is that why *Alice* was banned?"

The Secretary smiled. "There was no need to get to that point."

"What point?"

"The point where interpretation was necessary."

He stared at the old man's face, willing him to explain.

"The book violates the rules by the admission of a talking cat, and a rabbit holding a pocket watch, and a caterpillar who asks existential questions and smokes a hookah."

How could he have missed it? They had banned *Alice in Wonderland* because it contradicted "sound logic." But the book only grew stronger, and started to spew white rabbits into the rooms and corridors of the Authority. Despicable creatures. Every day they were there to lure the censors down the rabbit hole.

"And when *do* matters reach the point where interpretation is required?"

"It rarely happens. Books generally don't make it past *The Manual for Correct Reading*."

"Then why was *The Interpretation Manual* created?"

"I think it was written as a means of preventing evil, just *in case* something happened, but it's never been used. Let's just say the Authority has no need whatsoever for interpretation."

Suddenly needing to get away, the new censor turned his back on the Secretary and left in a hurry.

He wasn't upset because the book was banned—only a fool would think that the System was wrong—he only wished he could have been the first to ban such a book. It was like being excluded from the most wonderful party in the world! He knew that as long as he remained a novice censor at the bottom of the food chain, he'd never get to read any more novels. Those delights were restricted to senior censors. They were the only ones allowed near the forbidden tree.

When his wife opened the bedroom door, he was still sprawled out on the floor after his very long, very slow fall in the dream whose walls were made of bookshelves. Books were digging into his back, his neck, his ankles, but he couldn't find the strength to get up. "Another dream?" his wife snorted.

Making do with a nod in response, he reached out so she could help pull him up. He sat down on the edge of the bed while his wife remained standing, rubbing hard at her fingers. That's what she did when she was scared.

"Revolution Day's coming up."

"I know."

"The little one doesn't want to go to school."

"Of course she doesn't," he said, squirming. Being a government employee, he hardly noticed celebration days. Naturally, he would see pictures of the President on the walls, and in the streets, and some extra flags would fly. And on the radio, he'd hear about the origins of the Party's Principles and Positive Realism's historical triumph over democracy after the bloody war. But that was the extent of it. As for schools, they took these occasions very seriously. They spent a week rehearsing, canceling classes, and devoting themselves to planning dances that would be performed on stage, in front of party big shots and the President.

"Maybe she shouldn't go," his wife continued.

"What do you mean?"

"What if she sees a blown-up photograph of the President in the schoolyard? Last year there was that whole scene. She's scared stiff of it."

He buried his face in his hands, resting his elbows on his thighs. In spite of himself, he imagined his daughter in the schoolyard, where they saluted the flag every morning. She was screaming and pointing at the picture, and there wasn't a single teacher in school who cared enough to cover the little one's eyes and give her a hug.

He sighed. "It needs to stop happening."

"I don't know how to stop it," his wife choked out, her voice hoarse with tears.

"The picture's going to stay up for the whole week, you know. She can't miss school for that long."

"But what if they laugh at her? What if they call her names, or—worse—what if they report us to social services? Say we're not raising her properly? Do you know what happens to children with symptoms like that? Do you know what happens to their parents?"

Yes, he knew.

Rehabilitation centers. Not just for the child, but for the parents. Long sessions of hypnotherapy and neurolinguistic programming and a crash course on the history of the System and the Party's philosophy, all wrapped up in the principles of citizenship. The aim? To instill in the participants a complete sense of belonging. But he had never seen himself as lacking a sense of belonging—the government didn't need to worry about him! Even his white lies didn't harm anyone. It's not as if he had started approving dangerous books. But the child. She would never survive in that place. It would kill her. He would be asked, over and over again: *Why didn't you report your child's condition earlier? Why didn't you have her examined?* And he wouldn't know where to start.

He sighed and buried his face in his hands again. "I'm so tired."

His wife sat down next to him and he felt the warmth of her body, inhaled the fragrance of her skin. *Before Zorba*, he thought, *I never used to notice such things.* He wanted to rest his head on her shoulder, but she was rubbing her fingers again and her voice was trembling. "Maybe we should take her to the doctor's, get a diagnosis—anything to explain this fear of hers. And then we won't look like failures or, or traitors—"

"If we take her to the doctor's, he'll send her to a rehabilitation center."

"They'll try treating her at home before it comes to that."

"You know she's not afraid of the President, it's just his picture. And there's no end to things she's afraid of. Skyscrapers, full moons, flags. I took her to a plant shop and she started screaming because of some strange black blobs on the back of a fern leaf. That can hardly be called a crime!"

He stopped talking for a moment, then spoke slowly. "She—is—not—sick."

"Yes, she is."

"She's got an imagination. What child doesn't? It's a vestige of the Old World, like a tailbone. You don't see people walking around with tails dragging behind them, do you? Her symptoms will fade when she goes to elementary school—they'll take care of it. It's what they do."

"And what about Revolution Day?"

"Tell the school she's got chicken pox or something."

His wife was about to get up when the child ran in wearing a pink princess costume and shiny red shoes as if it were still Purification Day. Her hair was streaked with baby powder fairy dust and she was hugging a stuffed wolf to her chest.

"Baba?"

A strange pain gripped him. Everything she did alarmed him and everything he had done to help her exist in this world had failed. Utterly. He was standing firm on one side of reality, where a thing could only be itself, and he could feel her rejecting both him and what he knew to be true. She wanted to cross over to the other side where people walked upside down and everything was not what it was. Forcing a smile, he pulled her onto his knee and kissed her hair, gently pinching her cheek. "Are you glad you're getting a holiday?"

She nodded, happy to be sitting on his lap while her mother stroked her hair.

But his wife suddenly snatched her hand away and stood up. "Who's going to take care of her all week?"

"What do you mean?"

"I don't have any vacation days left."

"Well, I don't have any annual leave yet, you know that. I haven't been there for a full year."

"What are we going to do?"

2

HE COULDN'T imagine a worse situation—even though it was forbidden to do so at all. And he couldn't stop himself from imagining his daughter wandering the corridors of the Censorship Authority like a picture-book character on the loose. She knew so many stories—he'd never understood how—and she somehow managed to embody each of their protagonists. They were stories he hadn't told her, stories he didn't quite remember, and yet he found them strangely familiar. He had decided that the only logical explanation was that she'd thought up the stories herself: tales of fairy dust and the boy who could fly, the wicked witch and the magic shoes, and the poisoned apple too. She was like a house possessed by spirits, the final doorway to the past.

Had Wonderland, or wherever it was that stories came from, recruited his daughter for some kind of plot to overthrow the government? Was it trying to use her to come back to the real world? Like a metaphor, or a conduit for meaning? Perhaps the child was made of the dark matter that fills the universe, no different from a black hole that allows elements to travel through time and space, confounding humanity to no end. But people can only travel through time in stories. He knew this, but his daughter didn't. The books must be trying to get even with him, not because he was working on banning them—they paid no mind to that—but because he'd read them. The books wanted to take over his world.

He was in too deep. Whoever read a book was never the same. Suspicions against him would mount. Book censors, even more than others, were required to be immune to imagination.

The child wouldn't let him or her mother brush the fairy dust out of her hair, or take off her shiny red shoes. She said she wouldn't be able to find her way to the Emerald City without them. It left him off-kilter to hear such gibberish. Normal—that's how she needed to look. Clad in her khaki uniform, as though this was an ordinary absence from school— something that could happen in any family—and not a suspicious attempt to escape the Revolution Day celebrations.

But it was getting late and she was still lying on the floor, flailing and screeching. He couldn't get her under control and he needed to get to work on time. Otherwise, he'd be slapped with a fine. All the other children barely had tailbones, but she was like a long-tailed monkey. As soon as she walked with him into the censors' office, everyone would see it—of this he was certain. And he had no idea how to hide her imagination. How could anyone conceal something so powerful? But she had to come with him, at least for today, until his wife found a way to get out of work for the rest of the week.

Beads of sweat formed as he drove to the office, staring blankly at the road. The damp patches under his arms grew darker on his clothes.

When they drove down streets flanked by giant skyscrapers, he asked the little one to close her eyes—the last thing they needed was another panic attack. Would someone inform on a child? The receptionist, perhaps, or the door attendant. Maybe the First Censor. One of them might call the emergency hotline to report a child showing signs of familial neglect, and the Childhood Protection Society would come and take her to a rehabilitation center. Years ago, a distant cousin of his had lost a daughter there. She was taken to the center and never came out. Her case had been too advanced for the treatment to work, they said. She hadn't survived. They had given him a set of instructions, telling him how to get past the pain and return to the path of Positive Realism. Having more children was the fastest and most effective cure for grief, they said. They advised him to start volunteering, to work longer hours. His cousin now had four children, all of whom wore khaki and loved school and went to Scouts. They were perfect children with their eyes on the future. Not a tail in sight.

He hadn't doubted it for a second. All the news about the exceptional success that government labs had achieved in the field of developmental studies. Imagination had truly begun to shrivel and fade away, proving that if you control a human being's circumstances, you can drive their development in a certain direction. You can encourage the existence of New

Humans with no imagination and extremely limited desires, and without any pesky existential musings.

It was almost impossible not to love a government that worked so hard to make you happy. And who was he to break the System's rules? He'd always believed that the System knew what it was doing, that it was there for his sake. And he was sure that his mind was free from the impure dregs of the Old World. From revolutionary thoughts of any kind. He had never—to the best of his knowledge—been a fan of democracy or the digital revolution. In that age, foolishness was exported far and wide. Everyone had knowledge, so everyone had power. He didn't want to return to those times; the world was much simpler the way it was now. But he couldn't bear to lose his child. There was no way she could be one of those Cancers the government issued warnings about—she was only five years old! Given time, she'd learn the right way to live. Yes, they only needed to give her a little more time.

He started to rock in his seat. His legs were weak. He had never been so terrified in his life—he didn't even react when he saw a disturbed man dancing barefoot on the sidewalk. His daughter was in the back seat, talking to her stuffed wolf about the grandma it had eaten. The wolf was saying the grandma had been delicious. The new censor decided to interrupt this ridiculous conversation. He needed to prepare her.

"Baba needs you to help him with a few things," he said. "If anyone asks you why you're not at school today, tell them your tummy hurts."

"But it doesn't hurt."

"Pretend it does."

He could hardly believe what he was asking his child to do. What kind of father was he? He bit his lower lip. He really was in trouble now.

"The grandma is in my tummy now, and she's kicking me!" complained his daughter.

"Yes, yes, but don't you dare say anything like that in front of other people. And if anyone asks why you're wearing a princess costume, or why you've got powder all over your hair—"

"It's fairy dust."

"—tell them that your good clothes are in the wash and that Mama didn't clean them yesterday because she was sick."

"And why didn't you wash them, Baba?"

"Because the washing machine's not working."

She nodded slowly, confused by his instructions. "I thought you worked somewhere fun." She wiped her sweaty palms on her lap.

"Who told you that?"

"The rabbit."

What nonsense! The rabbits hadn't shown up at his house yet, had they? She was just imagining things. Yesterday, some cat told her to throw an entire grilled chicken in the trash. The day before, she was talking to the pigeons. And the day before that she'd been trying to make friends with a ladybug! All this silliness would gradually fizzle out. One day it would disappear forever.

3

LIGHTHEADED, he approached the entrance to the Censorship Authority holding his daughter's hand. He could see the alarm in the eyes of other employees, as if his child were walking around barefoot. Looks of condemnation. Strained smiles. Even the janitor was standoffish. He was a failure as a father, a threat to the fabric of society. If only his daughter really did have superpowers and could turn herself invisible. That would take care of everything. But reality was a brick wall: firm and unwavering. All the same, if reality was so unavoidable, then why didn't it stop her?

His fingers slick with perspiration, he gripped her arm and they kept walking. He greeted everyone and smiled as he never had before—he was reminded of the Secretary and silently cursed the old man. He had to make everyone comfortable. Any one of them could pick up the phone and report his monkey-child in a second. He had never before pressed a tip into the janitor's hand, nor told the receptionist that the brown frames of her spectacles brought out the color of her eyes. As for that man from Administrative Affairs he'd passed in the corridor, he hadn't let him pass without telling him he looked like he'd lost at least five pounds, even though the man was a mammoth. His daughter wanted to run down the long hall upon sight of a rabbit at the other end, but he dragged her to the censors' room. Seven wooden puppets pulled their heads out of their books and stared at the child. Not one of them had the decency to blink. He felt like a Neanderthal on the run from the Natural History Museum. But in spite of all this, he injected an extra dose of cheerfulness into his expression—a first.

"Good morning!"

"Is that your daughter?" asked the Second Censor. Nothing more.

Not one of them dared to say *She's sweet*, or *What are you wearing, child?* or *Why aren't you in school?* or anything else. They must have been staring at her long monkey's tail. Making the most of their shock, he took charge of the situation.

"Sorry I'm late," he mumbled. "It's my daughter. She was complaining about her stomach this morning, and her mother's at work. I had to—"

The First Censor nodded. "And how's the child feeling now?"

"Er. She's a bit better, I think. We have a doctor's appointment this afternoon, but—"

"Is she spending the rest of the day with you?"

"I think so. She won't bother us. I can give her some picture books to keep her busy. We have children's books here, don't we? Who inspects them?"

"The Children's Book Censorship department on the fourth floor."

"Thank you!"

Steering his daughter away, he left the room and sighed in relief. Everything was under control—he wouldn't let them ask any more questions. Adrenaline pumping, he proudly stroked her head. "What a smart girl you are! Let's go and find you some stories."

He took a few steps toward the elevator. Never having gone above the first floor, he hadn't had the chance to wander around the Authority's other departments. Perhaps this was the perfect time to venture into that giant eye censoring books, movies, television, plays, documents, newspapers, magazines—everything that humankind could possibly produce. All of it was subjected to strict and rigorous review, which was ultimately meant to bring him the greatest happiness. The State's slogans filled his head, just like the words of *Alice* and *Zorba*.

But his daughter suddenly slipped her hand out of his and pointed to the end of the corridor, shouting, "Baba! The rabbit! There he is!" She ran after it, clattering down the marble hall in her red shoes. He was sure she'd stepped in one or two droppings along the way.

"Come back here!" he yelled, but she didn't listen. He knew where the rabbits would go: first to the Secretary's room, and from there to the Department Head's office. This was getting out of hand. *Damn that old man! Damn him and his rabbits!* He ran after the child, holding out his arms. "Come here, darling, come here! No running! You'll fall!" But she had already turned the corner, and he was certain she would find the old man crouching on one knee, feeding a rabbit.

When he caught up with his daughter, she was standing with the tip of her braid in her mouth, chewing on it, and admiring the Secretary, who—exactly as he'd expected—was feeding a lettuce leaf to a rabbit. The old man peered at the little girl. He had a mysterious twinkle in his eye, as if he'd been waiting for her. "And who do we have here?" he murmured.

She giggled.

"I know you," said the Secretary, coming closer to her, kneeling down, and removing his spectacles. "I recognized you from your shoes!" More giggles. "So, tell me. Have you found her yet?"

"Found who?" interrupted the Book Censor.

The old man looked up at him, incredulous. "Who else would it be? The Wicked Witch of the West! Ask your daughter, she knows."

Nodding, the child said, "She's dead."

The Secretary pinched her cheek. "That's wonderful news. Now we can live in peace. What beautiful clothes you're wearing! A real princess! If we hid a pea under forty mattresses, you'd still know it was there, wouldn't you?"

She nodded again, her cheeks going pink.

"So, what brings you here? Did you follow the rabbit?"

The new censor felt his blood run cold when he saw the fascination in his daughter's eyes, unable to believe that someone in this world understood her so well.

"You're a good girl. Children are wonderful. They always know what has to be done. They follow the rabbits without being stubborn about it." The Secretary glanced at the new censor, squinting his eyes in reproach.

The child beamed. "I know who you are, too," she said.

The old man nodded. "I know, I know, I'm famous." Then he looked up at the new censor. "What are we going to do?"

"What's it got to do with you?"

"The Department Head will be here any minute."

The new censor chewed the inside of his cheek. "We were going to the fourth floor—"

"For children's books?"

"Yes."

The old man sighed. "You won't find a single book there that's fit for reading."

"What do you mean?"

"They don't inspect children's books anymore. They stopped importing them because they're littered with destructive values and remnants of the pre-Revolution world. Now the department writes them instead. They've hired writers and illustrators to produce books that mostly talk about—"

"—the Revolution?"

"Exactly."

"And do they have pictures of—"

"Of course they do."

The Secretary looked at the little girl and smiled. Turning to the new censor, he said, "This is going to be a problem, isn't it?"

4

THE CHATTER went quiet as soon as he returned to the seven censors' office. He was clearly the topic of the day. But he painted a Cheshire Cat's grin on his face, even as his head suddenly filled with voices.

> "*Would you tell me, please, which way I ought to go from here?*"
>> "*That depends a good deal on where you want to get to.*"
>> "*I don't much care where—*"
>> "*Then it doesn't matter which way you go.*"

The words of the novel floated in his head, encroaching on his world. He felt smothered. Contained. Imagination would always find minuscule pores in the delicate skin of reality—he knew that now. It would squeeze its way through to the surface. He tried to ignore the fact that he'd just come up with a completely mad metaphor, and then he remembered the cat's words: *We're all mad here.* At his desk, he picked up a book for inspection. He was in a vindictive mood and felt like banning a hundred books.

The seven censors tried to be kind—within reason, of course. They displayed the exact amount of consideration they must have guessed would be appropriate for a father going through the pain of raising a child who doesn't want to wear beige like everyone else.

"Oh, it's you." The First Censor smiled, which he normally never did.

We can't help it, the new censor thought. *Whichever way we go, we'll find ourselves among mad people.* He wondered again if these were his thoughts, or Alice's, or the Cheshire Cat's.

"Where's the little one?" asked the First Censor.

He was about to say she was with the Secretary, but he was afraid that instead of being branded an "unfortunate father," he'd be known—at the very least—as a "negligent father." If things were given their proper names, he'd be labeled a "traitor." *What was I thinking? How could I have let her stay with him? He's a—*

His armpits were damp again.

"She's with one of the nice ladies on the fourth floor."

The First Censor nodded.

Good, he thought. *They probably think those new books will be able to fix her.*

Silence came over the room once more, and they all pretended to return to their inspections. For the first time since he was hired, the new censor felt that he was a part of the overarching rhythm that bound the censors to one another; they were partners in the profession. Together, we will confront imagination's monsters and guard the surface of the world!

Was he risking his daughter's safety by leaving her with the Secretary in the storeroom, with all those picture books the old man had somehow held on to? That man was a walking, talking cancer cell polluting his daughter's thoughts. All those stories about princesses and peas and the Wicked Witch of the West. What if he—

A chill crept into his limbs. His eyes glazed over. He couldn't read a single line. But he had to turn the page, otherwise everyone would know he wasn't working. Besides, he couldn't have missed anything important—the book was about conversation skills between married couples, something that the System wasn't too concerned about. But shouldn't he check on his daughter? Just for a minute?

Before he could stand up to leave, the First Censor began what felt like a staged conversation with the Second Censor, and he was forced to be their audience.

"Children. They're wonderful, aren't they?"

"Yes, the best."

"It's not easy being a father."

"No, of course not. It takes experience. It's always easier with the second child. You know what to do by then."

"You're right. My brother's daughter was very sensitive and had some worrying symptoms. Imaginary friends, you know—that sort of thing. But he handled it, cured her completely."

"Really? Did he take her to a rehabilitation center?"

"No, there was no need to go that far. Every night, the family would gather in front of the TV, and they'd watch documentaries produced by the Authority. They're very useful programs and they can correct a lot of wrong thinking."

"Can imagination really be cured like that?"

"If you saw the girl today, you'd never guess she'd been sick. Unbelievably effective!"

He couldn't listen to another word. His knees were knocking together and the Cheshire Cat's grin was slipping from his face. He wanted to scream. Instead, he got up and said, "Excuse me, I need to go to the bathroom."

He could hear the little one's giggles from a distance. In the storeroom, he found the old man with his ear on her stomach. "Wow! That's some kicking!" he said.

"I told you this grandma kicks and she never sleeps. She's just like the seven goats in the wolf's belly. They kicked a lot too."

Dozens of picture books were scattered across the floor, full of witches, dragons, woods, wolves, and houses made of gingerbread and candy. When the little girl noticed her father, she ran to hug him as if he'd been away for an eternity. "Baba!"

He hugged her back, unable to believe that he was touching her, that the books hadn't swallowed her whole, that she hadn't turned into a mere figment of his imagination. "Did you miss me?"

"That was quick. How many books did you ban in half an hour?" asked the Secretary.

"I came to take the child," he said tersely.

"To the department? Are you mad?"

"You're polluting her mind."

"She's the only unpolluted thing in this place."

"You're talking like a traitor."

The old man looked dejected but managed a smile. He took off his spectacles and pressed the pads of his fingers to his eyelids. "I have nothing to lose," he said softly.

For the first time, the Secretary appeared free of his usual unexplained happiness. He seemed spiritless—perhaps even depressed. The new censor took comfort in this, and decided to threaten him. "You'll lose the books. The Department Head's library. There won't be anything like that to read in prison, you know."

The old man looked up at him, his eyes cloudy, a sad half-smile on his lips. He whispered, "Everything I do is for the sake of—"

"The child—"

"—that library."

"You're mad!"

"We're all mad here."

5

THE CHILD didn't want to leave, and the new censor found himself sitting on the floor, staring at the picture books that filled the space around them. His daughter was lying on her stomach, open book between her hands, swinging her legs in the air. She was looking at an illustration of a wooden puppet walking down the road with an elegantly dressed cricket.

"Where did you get all these books?"

He couldn't stop himself. If the Authority had banned all imports of children's books, then where had these come from?

The old man dusted his hands off. "I can teach you everything I know," he said.

"What do you mean?"

"Where to find books. Where to hide them. How to erase all traces of them from the records, to make it seem as if they'd never been written. I can be your guide to—"

The new censor interrupted him. "You haven't answered my question."

"I rescued them."

"What do you mean?"

"The books were on death row."

"I don't understand."

He suddenly regretted asking so many questions. His curiosity had brought him to the darkest corners of the earth. And, since it was forbidden, nobody had ever imagined what went on in those dark places. They were murdering books! His breath quickened and the walls seemed to be closing in. He thought of Zorba, but this time he wasn't on the island, dancing barefoot on the beach with his arms reaching out toward the sea. His hands were shackled, and again there he was on an ancient tumbrel pulled by an aging horse, being taken to the guillotine.

It was the best of times, it was the worst of times . . . it was the season of Light, it was the season of Darkness, it was the spring of hope, it was the winter of despair . . . we were all going direct to Heaven, we were all going direct the other way.

Words swarmed his mind. Yet another book he'd read on the sly. He'd found it in one of the "banned" boxes. It was timeworn with yellowed pages that threatened to fall apart in his hands at any minute. And because he recognized these things now, he clearly remembered that the novel—about a guillotine and the people who had been sentenced to it during the best and worst of times—didn't make a single noise when he turned its pages, not necessarily because the paper was worn out, but because it was scared. The book didn't want anyone to know it was there. If it were destroyed, everyone who'd survived in the story would be gone too. There would be no one left to remember the ones who had died. The balance of the world goes horribly askew when a story is confiscated; it becomes a darker, more ominous place.

Can these thoughts possibly be my own? he asked himself. He hadn't heard Alice's voice in his head, or even Zorba's.

"What did you think they do with books that are banned?" whispered the old man.

The Book Censor looked away. "I can't imagine."

"I'm not surprised."

"I don't want to kn—"

"They take them to the Pyre."

He didn't know why the Secretary was whispering. Was he worried the child might hear? The Book Censor wasn't worried about his daughter, who stared down imaginary dragons and kept a wolf in her wardrobe. She wouldn't be afraid of a Book Pyre. But his own heart fluttered in his chest.

"Why are you whispering?"

"There's no need for you-know-who to find out."

"The child?"

"The books."

The new censor laughed, unconvinced. "The books know everything," he said.

"Nearly everything, yes. But these books . . . They're just children's books."

"They're full of dragons, and gray-haired old witches—"

"—and happily-ever-afters?"

"Isn't it always happily ever after?"

The old man sighed. "We've locked ourselves in a storeroom with a child, just so we can read *Little Red Riding Hood*. All the happiness in this world has been defeated a long time ago."

The new censor looked around. He'd almost forgotten how reckless the situation was. He wasn't standing alone with a book he'd picked up by chance from one of the boxes. He was consorting with a traitor to the System, a monkey-girl in shiny red shoes, and dozens of stolen picture books that should have been burned.

"What if someone sees us?" he asked.

"I paid the janitor to stand guard at the door."

"Does he know what we're doing in here?"

"He doesn't want to know. The cash was more than enough."

"But do you trust him?"

"I trust the power of money. It's magical."

The old man winked, making the new censor wonder how his mood could have improved so quickly after discussing the crushing defeat of everything that was good. Then, plucking up his courage, he asked the Secretary the one question he'd avoided, panicked as he was.

"Have they burned *Zorba the Greek*?"

6

"NO, THEY HAVEN'T burned *Zorba*.

"Not yet, at least. They designate one day a year for burning books. You know it as Purification Day, and it hasn't come yet. Right now, *Zorba* is buried somewhere in the boxes lying around the holding pen. It'll be sent over to the warehouse soon."

The Pyre. Purification. And what on earth was this warehouse? He thought about hell—the figment that it was—and wondered if it was a matter of faulty wiring in his brain, this ability to imagine things that weren't there. Did it even matter that a word could mean more than one thing? But he didn't share his thoughts; this was possibly the first time he was certain they were his own. Instead, he only muttered that he didn't understand.

The old man sighed and rubbed his eyebrows. "What is it you don't understand? It's all too real, unfortunately. A practical problem that needs a practical solution. No system can keep a copy of every single book it's ever banned. They'd need thousands of acres of storage. Did you really think that the government would keep all those books as mementos?"

"Shh!" said the Book Censor. "Don't mention the government!"

The old man grinned. "You're a fast learner—for a new Cancer."

He bristled at the mere thought. What had he done to make the old man think he'd go to those lengths? "I am not a Cancer."

"My mistake," the old man replied lightly. They looked at each other.

"So what happens exactly?"

"They have to clear out enough storage space to make room for the freshly banned books. Those new books have one year to live, but the older, aging ones—they're burned first."

"What about the Department Head? How come he gets to keep the books he banned?" The question tumbled out before he could stop it.

"People who make the rules are allowed to break them."

"It's not fair."

The old man laughed, scratching his eyebrow. "He needs that library to motivate the Book Censors—or so he says."

"Do you believe him?"

"He and I have an understanding of sorts. We both want that library for different reasons. I don't need to know his motives."

"Why did he step in to keep you out of jail?"

"We have a history."

A full minute of silence reigned before the Book Censor found the nerve to break it. Hanging his head, he asked, "How many books are burned every year?"

"Depends on how many new ones come in."

He felt a darkness squeezing his lungs and thought, for the first time, that he didn't want to live in this world. It scared him. And even though, time and again, books had been presented to him as evil agents plotting to take over the world, and even though books had almost thrown him out of his house—not to mention biting his wife—he couldn't bear the thought of burning them. Banning them was punishment enough. He imagined what all those books imprisoned in the warehouse must be feeling as they waited for Purification Day. The aimless conversations with which they passed the time so they wouldn't have to think about the Pyre. No doubt they leaned on each other, steadying their shudders as they got carried to their death. Again the lines entered his head. *It was the worst of times* and *we had nothing before us*.

He looked at the books scattered on the floor around him and spotted *The Gingerbread House*, *The Princess and the Pea*, *The Magic Beanstalk*, and *Gulliver's Travels*. His heart shivered like a wet sparrow.

"Are these the only books that were saved from the Pyre?"

The old man's eyes glittered. "Hardly."

"Where do you hide them?"

"I've told you before: I can teach you everything I know. How to fool the System. How to save the books."

"Why would you do that?"

"My time is coming to an end. I won't leave behind thousands of orphaned books."

"And you want me to—?"

"Become the Guardian of the Library."

7

Who am I then? Tell me that first, and then, if I like being that person, I'll come up: if not, I'll stay down here till I'm somebody else.

I wonder if I've been changed in the night? Let me think: Was I the same when I got up this morning? I almost think I can remember feeling a little different.

Was it yesterday, or even the day before—before that book?

But if I'm not the same, the next question is, Who in the world am I?

His wife shook him gently. "You're talking in your sleep," she said.

She lay back down beside him and gently pulled his arm around her waist. It was her first night in their bed since the book had bitten her. She'd finally realized that the books weren't going anywhere anytime soon. And when, over the past few days, he'd begun to experience worrying symptoms at night—screaming, laughing, sleepwalking, even dancing—she knew she had to stay by his side in case something happened, and that the books had to accept her existence as reality. And reality was something that couldn't be pushed aside, even by a million books. His wife believed that. He wasn't sure anymore.

He hadn't been talking in his sleep. He'd been reading! Line after line of the words that Alice pumped into his head, words that had become his own. *Who am I?* He took his wife's hand and pressed it tightly to his chest. *Could she snuff out this cursed thing waking up inside me?* She thought he wanted to . . . "No. Not now. Go to sleep," he breathed.

She rested her head on his chest. That was better. He needed the weight, something to keep him anchored. He'd been floating, floating around for such a very long time in that deep, deep hole. Why couldn't he just glide through what he was reading? Why did he have to take every line to heart, allowing the words into the most intimate parts of his life, embedded in his panic attacks, his bed, even his daughter?

"Are you okay?" he heard his wife whisper. She was still awake. He hugged her closer, grateful to have her back. There was a gaping void in his chest that he knew his wife should've filled, but she was no match for it. It would swallow her up and send her off to the unknown. He didn't want to have to worry about her as well.

His eyes got used to the dark and he looked for a long time at the ever-growing stacks of books in front of him. He stared at the books, and the books stared back. "What are you waiting for?" they asked him. He was waiting to find out who he was. He knew who he had been before that book, but now he knew nothing. Was he a book censor or a reader? A guardian of surfaces or the Guardian of the Library? He had to choose, and he had to tell the Secretary what he'd decided.

He'd been avoiding the old man ever since their last conversation, even though his daughter mentioned him almost every day. Every morning she begged him to take her "to the place where stories went." According to her, the Secretary knew more stories than the grandma in the wolf's stomach. Perhaps he was the only person who had not punished her for being different. He probably even rewarded her for it. At the end of that day in the office, when the new censor was about to leave, he glimpsed true fear in the old man's eyes. "You must guard your ward well," he'd said.

Had he meant the library or the child? She was in danger here, yes. But what could he do about it? Where could he run when she was so visible? Colorful, bright, full of stories, trailed by an endless string of imaginary creatures. The new censor had sighed, hunched over. "Things will get better," he said. "She'll learn to adapt."

The Secretary pursed his lips and looked at the floor. "The worst thing that can happen to a child like this is to adapt." He gently pinched the little one's cheek. "Wait here for a quarter of an hour, then leave the storeroom. We shouldn't be seen together."

The new censor nodded. It was a sensible idea. They'd gone their separate ways. He no longer knew where he belonged. Who would tell him who he was? If he closed his eyes and dreamed that he was reading his thoughts, which were also Alice's thoughts, and if the Cheshire Cat showed him the way to the hookah-smoking Caterpillar and it asked him, "Who are you?"—what would he say?

I know who I used to be before that book. I was a guardian of surfaces, then I fell down the rabbit hole, he might answer. Maybe the Caterpillar would tell him that he was going to *turn into a chrysalis, and then after that into a butterfly*, and then it would give him a bit of mushroom. He'd grow from a guardian of surfaces into the Guardian of the Library, from a government employee into a traitor, from a good citizen into a Cancer who would one day be arrested because the System always won. They would take his daughter to a rehabilitation center. They'd try him for treason. Happy endings had been quashed long ago, and he knew this game well enough to not want to play it.

He was thinking about hell again. The word had been purged from the Holy Books—as well as all commentaries, study guides, and prayer books—when the government decided that religion must be based in reality, that there would be no more heaven or hell. They deconstructed all the symbols: Heaven was happiness and hell was misery. After the Revolution, the Party formed a committee of forward-thinking religious men and gave them the task of religious reform. Their aim was to relieve the texts of their inner meanings. In the end, you could read a Holy Book the same way you'd read the phone book.

He closed his eyes. His mind was made up. In the morning, he would tell the Secretary that he wouldn't become the Guardian of the Library, and that if the old man brought it up again, he would have no choice but to report him to the authorities. He would give *Alice in Wonderland* back, and he wouldn't even ask for *Zorba*. He would tell the old man to stay out of his life, not to speak to him or look at him again. And then everything would go back to its comfortable place on the surface of the world. He would read books that didn't say anything and fill libraries with them. And years from now, when he had received the required promotion and the necessary experience, and they'd officially allowed him to inspect novels, no book would affect him, even if it were *Zorba*. By then, he would have wrapped himself in a hard shell. He would be immune to meaning. His life would be normal, and he'd be a normal person, never wondering for a single second who he was.

8

BUT HE DIDN'T fall asleep.

He turned on the lights and asked his wife to leave. "Go and sleep next to the little one."

"But—"

"I need to work."

"Work?"

"Yes, work."

"It's three o'clock in the morning!"

"Please."

She wasn't happy when she left, but he didn't have time to explain. He turned the key twice in the door and began stacking the books into shopping bags and cardboard boxes—anything he could find. Book after book, he made up his mind to get rid of them all. He had always known, somehow, that it would end like this: It was either him or the books. Even the books wouldn't blame him for saving himself—he certainly couldn't return the favor. He would simply bring them back to the storerooms as if they'd never been gone.

He carried the heavy bags and boxes out to his car. His wife was in the living room blinking rapidly, her mouth wordlessly opening and closing, wondering what had gotten into him. "Where are you going with all those? To the Authority? Now? How will you get in, outside working hours?"

"I'll manage."

"Why now?"

"I have to return them. They belong to the government."

"Everything belongs to the government."

He thought of his daughter, her soulful little eyes and frail face, but banished the image from his mind as he hauled the last box into the back seat.

"I'm sorry," he whispered to the books, knowing what his decision meant. It meant they would be locked up in the warehouse for a year. After that—

He slammed the door. Why should he have to be a hero?

As he reached for the car door handle, he thought he glimpsed a fleeting shadow on the sidewalk. Lifting his gaze, he saw a man who appeared to be wandering aimlessly through the neighborhood's neat rows of houses. The stranger looked at him, so he turned away, feigning interest in something else. Upon turning back, he saw the man's lips part as if he had something to say. The Book Censor threw himself into the car, gunned the engine, and took off, every inch of his body shaking.

It was three o'clock in the morning. Nothing and no one went out walking at this hour except crickets and bats. Definitely not a man like that. The new censor told himself he was having delusions—it was understandable, he hadn't slept for days. He might suddenly think he was in a book. Or was it the book that was in him?

He sped all the way to the Authority and parked. A light was on in the security room at the entrance. He tapped on the window, waking the sleeping guard, who jumped out of his chair in a panic.

"I've forgotten some important papers in my office," the Book Censor claimed.

The guard rubbed his eyes and gaped at him in disbelief. "It's three o'clock in the morning."

"I'll be quick," he said, as he showed his badge. He was a man who knew himself—he wasn't going to lose himself in confusion again.

The guard nodded. "The door's already open."

But who had opened the door at an hour like this? "Is someone inside?" he asked.

The guard nodded, yawning. "He's taking inventory of the storerooms."

"Who?"

"I don't know," said the guard, indulging in a long stretch. "Probably that old man."

For some reason, the Censor wasn't afraid. It was as if he had already known what he would find on the other side of the door. As he walked through the marble corridors, he felt he was somewhere else. There were more rabbits than usual, and the smell of cabbage was even more pungent. Strange music flowed from somewhere. *I should have known it was the old man*. He marched straight toward the familiar office. The Secretary had been waiting for him all along!

Waiting for him here, every night. Just waiting for him to throw all caution to the wind and come back for more books.

Walking to the end of the corridor, he turned right and found the old man leaning back in his chair with his feet up on his desk, reading a book. There were seven white rabbits in the room; some were fast asleep, others were eating from a bucket of cabbage leaves. The Secretary's features lit up when he saw him. "So, you finally made it."

He found himself unsurprised by the old man's presence in the office at this hour, or by the rabbits, or by anything else for that matter. He was past all this madness. He'd come to put a stop to Wonderland.

"Yes," he said. "I came to return *Alice in Wonderland*."

The old man raised his eyebrows and swallowed hard. "Well, where is it then?" he asked the Censor.

"In the car, with the other books."

"The other books?" The old man slapped his thigh. "A natural Cancer."

"I told you before, I'm not a Cancer."

"What a waste of talent. Did you steal those books?"

"I was going to return them."

"When?"

"When I'd read them."

"And have you read them?"

"I don't want to read any more. You need to leave me alone."

"You're the one who followed the rabbits."

"They followed me."

"You know what's going to happen to those books, don't you?"

"I don't want to know."

"You already do!"

"What *you* already know is that I have a daughter. If something happens to me—"

"That wouldn't be the worst turn of events."

"What do you mean?"

"What if nothing happens? What if everything goes on the way it is?"

He thought of his daughter again. How would she survive the way things were?

The old man stretched out his arms and yawned. "I spent all night in the storerooms just for you."

"For me?"

"I was looking for *Zorba the Greek*."

The Censor's chest tightened. He clenched his teeth, digging his nails into his palms. He mustn't ask the question.

"Did you find it?"

"What do you think? Can't you tell we're celebrating?" He nodded at the rabbits nibbling their leaves as he opened a desk drawer. The novel had a blue cover with the shadow of a dancing man on it. The very same shadow. "We were happy about it," said the Secretary.

"About *Zorba*?"

"We thought you were going to save it from the Pyre, that we wouldn't have to worry about it anymore." He gently stroked the book, as if it was a puppy. "What a shame," he muttered.

But the new censor had gone from the room, leaving behind *Zorba*, the old man, the rabbits, and the music. He headed for the storeroom to find a trolley for the books. With a bit of grit and determination, he would transform himself from a reader into a book censor, from softhearted to stonehearted, from a butterfly into a caterpillar. It could be done. A person could behave as if he hadn't been reborn, rewind his memory to the moment before he'd met the man who danced on the island. But what if nothing happened? What if everything continued the way it was?

He pushed the trolley toward the car, but the books shrieked in his ears, all mixed together. He felt like a witness to inevitable massacre: arms, legs, children, old people—all turned to ash.

His cheeks grew wet. *What if everything goes on the way it is?* He was sobbing uncontrollably now, wiping his eyes and nose with the edge of his sleeve as he stacked the boxes onto the trolley, one after another.

He ran his fingers over the spines. *Tell me who I am!* he wanted to scream, but he knew that these books would never give him answers. Only more questions.

He heard footsteps behind him. "Is that you?"

"Who else would it be?"

It was the Secretary.

"I thought you were Zorba."

The old man smiled. "He wouldn't like it here," he muttered.

"What are we going to do?"

"About *Zorba*?"

"No—" He felt his voice shake. "How do I become the Guardian of the Library?"

BIG BROTHER'S
REPUBLIC

1

But it was all right, everything was all right, the struggle was fin-
ished. He had won the victory over himself. He loved Big Brother.

He read the last line and slammed the book shut. He hid it
in the bottom drawer of his nightstand, beneath other books,
scraps of paper, medicine boxes, anything he could find to
bury it. Then he burrowed under the covers, trembling. There
was no doubt about it; the book he had just read was evil, and
nothing would ever be the same again.

The words were quivering inside him, like seedlings breaking through dry earth. A thought popped into his head: If he
forgot to close the book, left it open on some page or other,
Big Brother might slip out. The notion made his lips curve
upwards. Something like that must have happened already,
many years ago—how else could this city be explained? The
Secretary had told him he couldn't become a Guardian of the
Library until he'd read that book. "It's just one book," he said,
"but it's like nothing you've read before. This is the mother
of all banned books. Listen carefully. They might catch you

reading a banned book and make you pledge never to do it again. But not this one. If you get caught with this book, you'll disappear. You won't exist anymore. It'll be as if you were never there in the first place."

At that point, he'd yet to read a single line. "But why?" he asked.

"Because it tells our story."

Fingers shaking, the Secretary slowly reached for the book to give to him. He had replaced the cover with one from a book published by the Censorship Authority titled *Latest Achievements in Genetic Evolution*. The new censor noticed the old man's fear. Taking the book, he stuffed it under his arm and turned to leave.

"Have you gone mad?" The Secretary's words stopped him short. "Don't walk around with it like that," he whispered. "Put it in a bag."

What was the point of having a fake cover if he had to hide the book?

The old man didn't give him a chance to ask. "Read it first, and *then* come back so we can talk. Don't come during the day. You need to be more careful now. Come at night. I'll be here."

Raising his eyebrows, the Censor asked, "Don't you ever sleep?"

"Do *you* sleep?"

He'd been under the impression that things had become so bizarre, nothing would surprise him anymore. After all, Wonderland had its own logic—or unlogic—but he hadn't realized he was about to leave Alice behind to enter the Republic of Big Brother. Now, as he cowered in bed, *he felt as though he were wandering in the forests of the sea bottom, lost in a monstrous world where he himself was the monster*. The slogans of the New World came back to him with unprecedented clarity:

WAR IS PEACE
FREEDOM IS SLAVERY
IGNORANCE IS STRENGTH

When he reached that point in his thoughts—or rather, in Big Brother's thoughts—he yearned for the days when Alice's voice was the only one in his head. Not even she could survive in the Republic of Big Brother. She'd end up flooding the world with tears because a thing was neither itself nor its opposite—it was whatever the government wanted it to be, and two plus two could never make four.

The clocks were striking thirteen when he finished the book, but he decided to wait another twelve hours before meeting with the Secretary. When darkness was complete, he found himself facing the Censorship Authority. He knew that he was, in fact, standing in front of the Ministry of Truth. Before, an invisible line—something like the equator—had separated the real from the imaginary, but after that book, the line ceased to exist.

A swirl of gritty dust swept in through the glass doors as he entered the building, and the hallway reeked of cabbage. Was it a smell from his memory, or from the book in his head? Or had it come from the Secretary's office, the hotbed of rabbits? It struck him then that he was a citizen of "that" Republic, an employee at the Ministry of Truth!

You're a thought criminal!

It was a child's voice, but it didn't sound like Alice. That's what became of children who didn't die in rehabilitation centers, he thought. They ended up guarding the surfaces of their neighborhoods, each of them in their own small way.

Surprisingly, the Secretary wasn't reading when the Censor arrived at his office. Instead, he was fiddling with a piece of bark. Where had it come from?

"What's that?"

"I used to be a carpenter before I came here," said the old man, gazing tenderly at the bark.

"You can't make anything with that."

"I know," he said wistfully. "I miss the smell. It smells of childhood, don't you think?"

The Book Censor thought the old man seemed deflated. Perhaps the System had finally wormed its way inside him. That's how systems worked after all: once embedded, they would devour you until there was nothing left, no different than a bunch of tapeworms. He thought of his daughter and wondered whether he had tried to force-feed her the government's larvae.

For a long while, the Secretary just stared at him, as if searching his face for traces of the book. Unmistakable bruising from the impact of learning the truth, contusions caused by words and sentences; the line separating fiction from reality had never really been there at all. He had begun to think like a Cancer!

"Are you having doubts?" the Secretary asked.

Then he rose to his feet and told the Book Censor to follow him.

2

HUMAN EXISTENCE IS SUFFERING.
THE ROOT OF SUFFERING IS DESIRE.
THE ROOT OF DESIRE IS IMAGINATION.

This time, it was the System's voice blasting inside his head. A sonorous broadcasting voice that rolled each syllable around on its tongue like the stone of a fruit, sometimes sucking it, other times spitting it out. A voice that pressed down on the words until they snapped like brittle twigs under military boots. The voice was the color of khaki and it had a mustache.

The only way he could make sense of the world anymore was through metaphor.

As he followed the frail old man through the dim hallways, he wondered if the Censorship Authority had surveillance cameras. But the Secretary didn't look worried—if they really were watching him, he'd have been thrown in prison years ago. In fact, he didn't understand how the old man had avoided arrest. What kind of security lapse allowed him to stay under the radar for so long?

Sometimes he still felt he was a model citizen, troubled by the government's disregard for matters of national security, and he'd forget that he belonged to a small Cancer cell trying to infiltrate the System. This reminded him of what he'd read in yesterday's book about "doublethink," but he immediately dismissed the notion—doublethink required you to deny its existence as much as it required you to acknowledge it.

Had he read about those things, or had he lived them? The New World was built on the idea of a human who could break free from the fateful pull of the past. His own upbringing at home and at school had taught him that there were three basic, legitimate desires: to belong, to procreate, and to work—everything else was toxic and superfluous. But had it succeeded? The early founders had focused their efforts on getting rid of unnecessary choices, arriving at the extremely simple (and truly ingenious) conclusion that human suffering and the worst of all human instincts were intimately connected to the ability to imagine. There was a time when robots were modeled after humans, but now it was the other way around.

Right from the start, the government had worked tirelessly to block all outlets of imagination, eliminating cognitive surplus, overturning the communications revolution, and abolishing what used to be known as the internet. Electricity was rationed, and sex was confined to a single, sanctioned formula: man, woman, and a marriage contract. Stores and restaurants dropped 80% of their product, and stocked only what was deemed necessary by the Ministry of Plenty. That wasn't its real name—it was the Ministry of Commerce—but he found it hard to disagree with the Secretary's conviction about the book he'd just read: it told their story. *Don't let your imagination run away with you*, he warned himself.

What would happen when everyone found out that the only person capable of understanding the truth was a five-year-old girl caked in baby powder?

The Censor walked quietly behind the Secretary, taking in his bony back and the dejected slope of his shoulders. *The old man must be tired of this game; maybe that's why he recruited me*, he thought. They headed for the storeroom where they'd had their first real conversation, surrounded by picture books, a little girl, a stuffed toy wolf, and an imaginary grandmother.

The old man sat cross-legged on the floor. The younger man sat facing him. He had made up his mind about hell: it was where the difference between what was real and what was imagined ceased to exist.

"Tell me," the old man began, then stopped to clear a strange hoarseness from his throat. "Do you know where the greatest library in the world can be found?"

He shook his head. How would he know? He'd never seen a proper library before in his life. Even bookstores didn't sell decent books anymore; they sold cigarettes, bottles of water, turkey sandwiches, and khaki pants. They were supermarkets that sold books alongside everything else, books full of soppy declarations, books that tried to teach their readers the secrets to happiness and success—books he had no interest in whatsoever.

As for the Department Head's library, he liked it well enough, but not to the extent that he'd think it was the greatest in the world. There must be a bigger one somewhere, even bigger than Victory Mansions, or the Ministry of Truth. A library that was dizzying, eternal, and in whose presence he might—with a little luck—lose consciousness, just like characters in the novels he'd read, when they encountered the Absolute. And it dawned on him then: a library was the closest thing humanity had to the idea of the Absolute.

He remembered that the Ministry of Truth contained three thousand rooms above ground level, and corresponding ramifications below. There were no other buildings in the city of similar size, except for rehabilitation centers. Not even the government laboratories came close. But the idea made his heart dance; his head filled with images of endless rooms packed with bookshelves. He'd felt this way once before: entering the wormhole, traveling through time, leaving his body, and inhabiting Zorba. He'd begun to understand what was happening to him in a different way, and his musings made him happy: seeing his thoughts—his *own* thoughts—made him feel wise and mature. Before turning those pages, he had been just a lonely book censor, but here he was, pondering the laws of physics and watching new galaxies unfurl in his head.

The universe was getting bigger, he was sure of it. What else could all these stories be doing with the world?

Even so, his answer was no—he didn't know where the greatest library in the world was. After all, he'd only just started to read, in a place where reading any truly meaningful book was a crime.

The old man tapped the side of his nose and gave him a sly wink. "It's the Book Detention Center."

His eyebrows shot up. "What? The Center where books are held captive until Hate Week? Er, I mean Purification Day? How—"

The old man interrupted. "Can you imagine what's inside there? All the banned literature in the world has passed through those walls. Every piece of writing ever produced by humankind. Hundreds of thousands, maybe even at one point millions, of books spread out over spacious acres." He swallowed. "All the world's treasures, buried."

This was some revelation! *They were sitting among boxes of books on which a deportation decision had been made—they would be taken to the world's greatest library.* He wanted to visit. To stand, small and vulnerable, among a sea of titles sentenced to death by execution. To inhale the musk of paper, dust, and wood, to hear the rustle of the browned pages, to run his fingers along the embossed titles on the leather covers and turn the books over in his hands.

"They call it the Labyrinth."

"Who?"

"Others like us."

"The Brotherhood?"

He knew the resistance called themselves Cancers, but were they really that different from the group in Big Brother's republic? A thought sprang into his head: every story was a retelling of older ones and a harbinger of tales still to come. It's been the same story since the beginning of time, and it will live on forever, giving birth to a new version of itself every day. He had never felt so close to understanding the Divine as he did at that moment.

"You can call them the Brotherhood, if you like."

How many Cancers were there? The question nagged at him, but he didn't ask. He liked knowing there were others out there besides this deranged, tree-hugging, book-smuggling old man who never slept.

"What do you Cancers want from me?"

The old man stared into his eyes. "We want you to sneak into the Labyrinth, grab some books, and bring them back."

He didn't understand. "You're asking me to go into a library where there is book after book and just pick some at random? What makes one book more worthy of saving than another?"

"You'll be given a list, of course."

"Based on what?"

Slipping off his spectacles, the old man glumly studied his shoes. "We're trying to save classics, fables, myths, folktales, songs from bygone civilizations, recipes for herbal medicines, old stories of creation, Holy Books in their original editions, and the commentaries written about them. Those get priority."

"Why?"

"Because they're changing the past, and we need to protect our collective memory. That way, when this world falls, as it's destined to do, we'll have somewhere to start from. Do you remember what the book said? *Who controls the past . . . controls the future: who controls the present controls the past.* We're trying to save the past to make the future possible." He paused. "But *you* clearly need to learn some history. You're a typical citizen in Big Brother's republic, stuck in a nation that's slowly killing you, trapped in the whale's belly, its stomach acid eating away at you, with no way to escape."

"And how can anyone escape from a whale's belly?" the Censor asked.

"By lighting a fire."

"But what will you do with the books we save? Where will you hide them?"

The old man's gaze wandered aimlessly again, a grin slowly forming on his lips. "Listen to this story," he said. "Once upon a time, there was a magic mirror. It belonged to a beautiful, slightly reckless princess. She had vowed never to be married, except to the young man who could hide from her mirror. The mirror could find anyone, anywhere; it was as good as any listening device, surveillance camera, or observation screen—and it could see everything, all the time.

"Whenever a man proposed to the princess, she would challenge him: 'Run away and hide from my mirror. If I don't find you before the night is over, come back the next day and we'll get married. But if I do find you . . .'" He drew a line across his neck with a finger and made a gagging sound.

The younger man gulped. "What happened?"

"Dozens of foolhardy suitors were executed until one came along who managed to give the magic mirror the slip. The princess dispatched her soldiers to every corner of the land, but the night went by and there was no sign of him. He had won. The princess was forced to marry him and be done with her murderous game. It was a great relief to her people."

"But where did he hide?"

"He hid in the princess's bedroom. He was right under her nose the whole time."

What was the old man trying to say? "What does this have to do with saving books?" he asked him.

"We'll hide the books in the Department Head's library."

"Are you out of your mind? He'll find out!"

"He won't suspect a thing."

"How do you know?"

"Because the idiot doesn't read. He just pretends to."

"But all those books—"

"Those are the books I read and approved myself. But after I got caught and they set up a committee to investigate, that impostor went and banned them all in one go. He held on to them as trophies. He only keeps them there to annoy me."

"And it never crossed his mind that you might be reading them in secret?"

"He probably knows."

"Then why hasn't he turned you in?"

"He needs me."

"What for?"

"I'm the one who understands him best."

"I don't get it."

"You don't need to."

From his pocket, the old man fished out a scrap of paper and shoved it into the Censor's hands—into the Guardian of the Library's hands. "Here's the list," he said. "One of our operatives will be waiting for you. Try not to get lost."

3

THE STREETS were empty, except for the occasional truck heading in the opposite direction. There were no lights and he couldn't make out the landscape around him, but he knew the silent hills scattered on both sides of the road.

The Labyrinth was a long drive from his house; he still had half an hour to go. His heart was beating a strange rhythm. He felt like a cheating husband meeting an old flame. His wife would never forgive him.

He'd turned off the lights before he left, telling his wife not to worry—he just needed to help take inventory of the storerooms. He stretched the lie even further, saying that the extra work came with extra pay, which meant he *might* be able to buy a dishwasher. He knew he was supposed to be careful not to raise his wife's expectations. Part of him still believed what the government preached: "Desire is the root of all suffering." Perhaps humans hadn't evolved in a way that emptied them of all desire; their desires had just been shaped differently. How else could he explain his wife's insistence on buying a dishwasher? His cravings for all those novels?

It was hard for him to comprehend the sheer abundance that had existed before the Revolution. A phone for every citizen: man, woman, and child! A camera in each phone, search engines to look up anything and everything, robots, all sorts of other madness. He'd always felt there was something wasteful about the whole thing, and he thought the government was justified in setting things right: banning cell phones from everyone except security personnel, introducing regular power cuts—not out of concern for the environment, but to limit people's options during their free time. His wife once told him that the latest figures showed how—over the past five years—electricity cuts had resulted in a fifty percent increase in birth rates. Apparently, the government needed more citizens. The unborn human being was more important than the living one; a fetus was closer to the ideal. As a result of the millions spent by labs pushing genetic development toward efficiency over cognitive skills, New Humans would now come into the world without any kind of tails at all. Perhaps one day people would even be born without tailbones, and that would be the System's greatest victory of all.

It was said that back in the days of cell phones, couples didn't so much as look at each other unless it was on a screen, but the old man didn't have much faith in those stories. "The government wouldn't ration technology just so people can have a happier marriage," he'd said. "Did you know that, in the twenty-first century, hundreds of thousands of cell phones were commandeered to make demands for democracy?"

"So that's how it was," the Censor had responded. "What a waste of time!" Rivers of blood were spilled in the name of democracy. Parliaments were filled with the worst possible human beings—drunkards, thieves, degenerates—all because people voted for them. He had never been a fan of the idea. But if all those people had demanded democracy, he didn't understand how the democracies could fall, giving birth to the New World.

The old man had smirked when he asked him. "That's because democracy was never truly established."

He had felt glad, then, that he would never know what the world had been like before the Revolution, and that nothing existed today that could prove—or disprove—any story about what had happened back then. "Systems built on brainwashing can transform you from a wooden puppet into a donkey," the Secretary had said. The Guardian of the Library didn't understand the metaphor, but he still found it funny. The government was working hard to change the past, *And yet the past, though of its nature alterable, never had been altered. Whatever was true now was true from everlasting to everlasting.* The book was droning in his head again.

That was why they'd made him a Guardian of the Library— to keep their collective memory from being bleached away in a world where brains were washed with the strongest of detergents. He sank his arms to his sides, keeping a limp grip on the steering wheel. *His mind slid away into the labyrinthine world of doublethink. To know and not to know, to be conscious of complete truthfulness while telling carefully constructed lies, to hold simultaneously two opinions which canceled out, knowing them to be contradictory and believing in both of them, to use logic against logic, to forget whatever it was necessary to forget, then to draw it back into memory again at the moment when it was needed, and then promptly to forget it again, consciously to induce unconsciousness, and then, once again, to become unconscious of the act of hypnosis you had just performed.* It was like believing that the earth was round and flat at the same time. He knew these lines by heart, even though he'd only read them once. His mind had become a magnet: words gathered like steel shavings in the twists and turns of his brain, constantly rearranging themselves into new formations. His head was filled with thoughts that didn't belong to him, and—truth be told—it didn't bother him one bit. Even when the voices got into scuffles and disagreements, and some of them began to scream, at least he wasn't lonely.

Half an hour later, he arrived at his destination: a car cemetery about a mile away from the Labyrinth. He turned the motor off and—just as the Secretary had instructed—went out into the night, walking between the skeletons scattered across the sprawling dirt lot, cars that used to run on fuel before they were replaced by electric ones. A faint light shone in the distant night. It was a mile away, perhaps a little farther.

He knew then in which direction the Labyrinth lay. He had found his path; now all that was left was to lose himself.

As he walked, he heard cats meowing and the odd fluttering noises of some bird—he couldn't tell what kind, it might have been a bat—and the thudding of his own footsteps. He knew this area; once a year on Purification Day, it filled with stands displaying goods from the Old World, now unwanted. It was on that day that the government proved it had won: The past had become nothing more than a kitschy museum. Any visitor who stole a look at yesterday's world wouldn't feel he'd missed anything at all.

Every year, the square was crowded with actors, acrobats, and displays of cell phones, tablets, laptops, cameras, compact discs, and other worthless junk. In another time, people might have visited museums to marvel at how advanced their ancestors were. Today, museums acquainted people with the backwardness of their past. All those misguided inventions, what had they achieved? And how could the world have imploded in the presence of all that knowledge? It had been an age of foolishness, and it was necessary to move beyond it into an age of wisdom.

For some reason, he remembered a phrase from the book, *Ignorance is Strength*, but ignorance was more likely a gentle, harmless power, no different from innocence. Once upon a time, he had been a guardian of the world's ignorant bliss, rescuing humanity from the ills of the cognitive surplus. Now, he'd crossed a line, bitten into the forbidden fruit. And since—according to the Secretary—the government knew it couldn't completely control people's desires, it gave them one day a year to indulge in impossible fantasies. To legally embrace every kind of recklessness. Drunkenness and debauchery were the order of the day; all semblance of dignity was abandoned. People in costume filled the square: monkeys, princesses, dragons, robots, knights, and pirates. Pointy-toed shoes, turbans, curved sabers, and fluffy skirts. Why did the government allow it, he'd always wondered, this annual trip to the past? Only to declare its defeat at the hands of the Revolution? It was his wife's favorite day, and his daughter's too. He bought all the little one's outlandish outfits from the makeshift stalls. Plus, there was the food—colorful candies, grilled corn on the cob, boiled chestnuts, caramel apples—so many choices, too many to consider. It made him tired just thinking about them.

Effigies of books were stacked on the ground, fake books made of cork that were used as fuel for the Purification fire. Government officials soaked them in kerosene and let them burn. They fed the fire with seven wooden effigies resembling people from certain groups: black-robed religious men, poets, novelists, long-bearded wizards in pointed hats, magicians with hidden playing cards in their pockets, paint-splattered artists, philosophers with crazed expressions, queers, and dissidents too. The people lit an enormous bonfire in which to burn their ancestors.

It occurred to him then that they didn't burn the real books in public, just the effigies. It was too much of a risk to bring such a huge number of banned books out into the streets, within easy reach of the masses. One curious person who picked up a volume and read a few lines could poison the entire society. So he'd stood with his daughter on his shoulders, cheering as the pages burned, while about a mile away, another fire blazed to incinerate real books. It struck him that a book was effectively the equivalent of a human being. But why did he love the strangeness and diversity of the characters and ideas he encountered in books, when the same things bothered him in real life? The government seemed to be more in tune with its thoughts than he was; it equally refused strangeness in both books and human beings. On the very first Purification Day after the Victorious Revolution, a real burning had been held—and neither books nor effigies had been its victims. But he wouldn't think about that now. People like him had the right to slip into the labyrinths of doublethink when reality was too terrifying to face.

4

THEN HE SAW the man who'd been waiting for him. He wore khaki pants, but his shirt was covered in blue and yellow stripes. He had a black-and-white checkered cloth wrapped around his head, his beard was unkempt, and—the newly anointed Guardian of the Library had to look twice in disbelief—his feet were bare! The man had been standing in the road in front of the entrance, waiting for him in the darkness of the dirt lot. He was brown-skinned with wide eyes and a tiny gap between his two front teeth. He was smiling, delighted to see the Guardian of the Library, and hooked his arm around his neck. Pulling him closer, he whispered, "Brother, where've you been all this time?"

The Guardian of the Library caught a whiff of something salty on the man's shirt. "Who are you?" he asked.

"Me? Don't you recognize me, Brother? I'm the Keeper of the Labyrinth."

"But how do I know you are who you say you are?"

The Keeper burst out laughing. "*Well, now that we have seen each other*," he said, "*if you'll believe in me, I'll believe in you. Is that a bargain?"* He nudged him with his elbow, and the Guardian recognized the words—they were from Alice's book! Stiffness melted away from his panic-stricken body and his limbs relaxed. He was elated to have met another reader.

They walked together. "Strange place," the man said. "Very strange. Not doing this for the rest of my life, I tell you. One day, I'll just quit. They can find someone else. I'm no hero—hate them, actually. Are you a hero, my friend? Hope not!"

The Guardian smiled. Someone else on this earth was neither tempted by the idea of being a hero nor thinking about fixing the world, but at the same time enjoyed breaking the rules. "What are you doing in the Labyrinth, then?" he asked.

"I'm only here for a short while, till they find someone else." He pointed at an enormous building, standing by itself at the far end of the lot.

The wide, pyramidal structure, windowless, dozens of stories high, was surrounded by fearsome iron fences punctuated with watchtowers. The whole thing was a bit dramatic, he thought. A book warehouse had no need for such tight security. They weren't going to escape anywhere, at least not without some help. But the thought of all those floors filled with new characters and stories he'd never heard of before made his head spin. "That whole—"

"What?"

"That whole building is just for storing books?"

The man shook his head. "All the old things are in there: cell phones, computers, tablets, compact discs. If it has to do with communication, they've got it. A research department, too—who knows what dark things go on in there. Labyrinth's in the basement. Books, books, and more books." His voice grew hoarse; he spoke of the books as if they were orphaned children. "It's bad, really bad down there. No one to pat their backs or tell them that it's all going to be okay."

In the dark, they walked silently until they drew close to the building, and then the Keeper's footsteps swerved as he nodded toward a side entrance. Taking two cards out of his pocket, he swiped them on a magnetic reader and the door opened at once. The Guardian couldn't believe it was that easy.

"Don't they have surveillance cameras?"

"You know the answer to that."

"What if they catch us?"

The man snorted. "Then we'll die and rest in peace."

They entered the building together, the Keeper's hand resting on his shoulder as if they were lifelong friends. The Guardian swallowed. He didn't want to die, even if he had committed a *thoughtcrime*. Why didn't the Keeper look afraid? Why didn't he pretend to be scared, if only to reassure him?

"Have you done this before?"

"Many times. You're not the first, and you won't be the last. Round it goes."

"Was anyone ever arrested?"

"Worry, worry, worry. We're Cancers! Hacking systems is our bread and butter. Don't worry—your mug will be erased from the recordings. About to piss yourself, eh?"

So that's why they called them Cancers! Because they spread everywhere, penetrating the system's joints, each from their own place without any one of them having to know the other. It was a cheering thought, knowing he wasn't all alone on the surface of the world, nor by himself beneath it. He wondered if the surveillance cameras at the Authority had also been hacked. They must have been—how else could the Secretary have survived all this time?

"Aren't you scared?"

"Fed up, more like it."

The man opened a door opposite the entrance and the Guardian saw a long dark passage that went on and on, an endless tunnel. He breathed in slowly. Taking a flashlight out of his pocket and switching it on, the Keeper walked ahead of him. The hallway was flanked on either side by countless closed doors.

"You said they have research centers here?"

"Mm-hmm."

"What are they working on?"

"Who knows? Probably a power-driven impaler."

"Are you joking?"

"Who really gets what goes on here? Looks like they're trying to bring back some of the old knowledge—you know, what was lost after the Revolution. Thermal cameras, fingerprint detectors, bugging devices—some say they're developing a private internet for the leadership. Technology is banned, except when it's designed to skewer the people." He snorted again. "You got a dishwasher back home?"

The Guardian thought of his wife and shook his head.

"Never mind. No one can buy one anyway."

The Keeper stopped in front of the last door, turned back to face him, and grinned. "You know the story of the pretty woman who popped out of a lemon?"

He shook his head but found himself licking his lips. "What pretty woman?"

The Keeper brought the fingers and thumb of his hand together and kissed them. "A beauty, a real beauty. This is how it goes:

"Once upon a time, a brave knight got hold of three magic lemons. Inside each lemon, he was told, there was a beautiful girl who would live for only a few seconds when she came out of the fruit before she would die of thirst. The only way to keep her alive was to give her a drink of water. The knight picked up a knife and cut the first lemon open. And what do you know, out came a woman so beautiful he could barely breathe. Paralyzed, he forgot to give her a glass of water, and, in a few short seconds, she faded away. He cursed, he swore, and vowed not to make the same mistake. But when he cut into the second lemon, he saw a woman even more beautiful than the first, and froze until the enchanting beauty disappeared. Again, he cursed, he swore, and slapped his own face.

He then decided to keep his eyes closed while he cut open the third lemon. He squeezed his lids shut, grabbed the knife, and cut the lemon in half, slicing off a chunk of his finger at the same time. As soon as he sensed the woman's presence, he handed her a glass of water without looking at her."

"And then what?"

"Then he opened his eyes."

"And was she beautiful?"

"The most beautiful woman he'd ever seen."

He winked and said, "Beware of the Labyrinth. Magic lemons are everywhere, and in each one there's a beauty who'll call for you to save her. But you must close your eyes. Keep them closed so you don't lose your way."

He opened the door. A staircase ran deep into the darkness. "Welcome to the Labyrinth, Brother."

5

THE GUARDIAN of the Library gasped.

He nearly fell to his knees.

He'd never seen anything like it. An infinite array of metal posts and shelves rose from floor to ceiling, crammed with rows of books, their little spines shoulder to shoulder, stamped with black-inked lettering: titles in fonts so small they were more like ciphers. Passages seemed to writhe and twist in all directions. And even though he stood at the bottom of a pyramid-shaped building, the spinning in his head made him feel like he was in a dome, never-ending and absolute.

It was a sprawling place; he couldn't see where it ended, and he definitely didn't know where it began. Each passage split into smaller offshoots, which in turn branched out themselves, again and again. The aisles were crisscrossed by bridges and packed with shelves—it might as well be a snakes and ladders board! He walked, as if possessed, between the magic lemon trees (the beautiful girls called to him, he could hear them so clearly!) without closing his eyes.

He wanted to tear off his clothes right then and there, to be naked, to dance like Zorba. Unable to believe that this forbidden fruit was his for the taking, he ran his fingers over the rows of books that extended, uninterrupted, on both sides. He had no doubt that the books had been written especially for him—he was the chosen one, and he'd finally arrived at the promised land. The books were practically vibrating. The thrill of it all sent him into a fit of booming laughter and he had to wipe tears from his eyes. Was it possible, after everything he'd been through, that heaven was right here in this nightmare of a place?

Picking up books at random from the shelves, he opened them and sank into their worlds. In each book, he found a parched beauty whose thirst only a reader could quench. The moment one beauty disappeared, another would replace her. They scuttled away from him like crabs hiding in the nooks and crannies of rocks under the sea, slithered out of his reach like elusive meanings, and—in the end—he failed to hold on to a single one. The Labyrinth had driven him mad. He cried with thirst while drowning in a river. No torment could be worse than this, this endless slipping of possibility through his fingers. It reminded him of the Mad Tea Party, where wine was offered to the thirsty when there wasn't any to begin with, and jam was provided for the hungry on any day but today. How could he be satisfied with rescuing just ten books and leaving thousands more behind? And why did he only have two small hands with which to carry them?

He'd forgotten about the strange man, the Keeper of the Labyrinth, until he heard him shouting. Turning, he found the man calling him from the top of a ladder. "Hey, come take a look from up here!"

It seemed like a good idea to inspect the Labyrinth from above. To take note of its perimeter and its edges. Maybe he'd be able to make sense of it all if he saw the end of these interminable bookshelves.

He climbed with difficulty, his feet unexpectedly clumsy. "Look at you!" the man said, pointing at his legs with a loud guffaw. "Your knees are knocking together! Have you fallen in love?" He laughed again, as if he'd rehearsed the joke. "Watch out, the Labyrinth has many lovers and is happy to swallow them all."

At that moment, the Guardian had stopped to look down at the library. It was a real labyrinth—there was no joke about it—except the walls were made of books. And what was that moving over there? And there too, and over there? Could it be? "Rabbits!" he yelled, pointing at every white rabbit he caught sight of—there were dozens of them. "They're rabbits!"

"Yes, yes," said the Keeper. "You can't miss them." He shook his head as if the Guardian's astonishment was completely unwarranted. "Let's go, time's running out," he urged.

They made their way down the rungs of the ladder. As soon as he got to the bottom, he felt as if everything was suddenly clear. He was meant to get lost—that was the purpose of the whole exercise. He found his hands brushing the surfaces of the books as he walked past them, touching each volume, hardly comprehending that all these books had been sentenced to death. And in spite of this harrowing truth, the place seemed oddly cheerful.

"So?" The other man's voice jolted him. "What do you need?"

"What?"

"Have the magic lemons pickled your brain? Give me the old man's list. Hurry!"

He'd almost forgotten that he was here on a mission. Focus. That's what he needed to do, in spite of the charm of this chamber of treasures. This place was dangerous, dangerous! It would swallow him whole, and then he'd be gone, as if he'd never existed. "Pretend you're Aladdin!" the Keeper instructed. "Find the magic lamp first, then fill your pockets with coins—if you can." A burst of maniacal laughter followed.

What is he going on about? He couldn't blame the man; anyone who spent his days in a maze like this would end up losing his mind. And at least one thing was clear: he needed to close his eyes if he wanted to save these beauties.

He took the scrap of paper from his pocket—a list of titles written in the Secretary's scrawl. For the first time since he'd met him, he felt he owed a lot to the old man. Though he was standing in a government basement with a barefoot near-lunatic, and despite being surrounded by condemned books, he was happy.

The task of searching for the books took many grueling hours, and no one was immune to getting lost in the Labyrinth—not even its Keeper, who was cursing and swearing as he searched the catalog and tried to locate the right shelves. "You know," he said, "they could have used the Dewey Decimal System like any respectable library, but they don't want anyone to forget that this place is a detention center." He was going around in circles, passing the same spot again and again, but said, "Don't worry, my memory is ironclad: I'll find them."

Growing tired of walking around, the Guardian sat on the floor and read while he waited. It wasn't fair to the rest of the books, he thought. What made one book deserve to be saved over another? Who decided its worth? And why couldn't he rescue the slim book of poetry he held in his hands? He had grown to love poetry.

After a while, he heard his guide murmuring, "Right, right. Why didn't you say so before?" The man was talking to a rabbit! He grabbed a book from the shelf, came back to the Guardian, and tossed it into his lap. "The last one. Hightail it out of here before trouble finds us. Tell the old carpenter I wore out my feet searching for his books."

The old carpenter? Why did he get the feeling that everyone—except him—knew the Secretary's history? He grabbed hold of the books: ten volumes thick as bricks, stacked on top of each other, half of which he held in his right hand and the other in his left. The old man had given him permission to save whatever books he wanted, as long as he finished his task, but he couldn't carry any more. And—just like the knight in the story—he cursed and swore because he hadn't kept his eyes shut.

"I want to come back tomorrow," he said, "with a cart and boxes and bags."

The Keeper gently patted him on the back. "Just tell the old man, he gives me the heads-up."

At the last minute, the Guardian decided he could rescue another book, just one: that little volume of poetry. He would clench it between his teeth and take it with him, far away from this death trap that was—impossibly—a sheer paradise.

6

INSIDE THE WOODEN wardrobe with the creaky hinges, behind a row of hanging khaki trousers, the Guardian of the Library installed a secret shelf. On it, he placed the first book he'd acquired for his private collection: *Zorba the Greek*, the novel that changed everything.

As time passed, and with every book-rescuing expedition, the library in his wardrobe grew. Every time he sneaked away to the Labyrinth, he'd give the Secretary the books he'd asked for, and the old man would place them on the shelves in the Department Head's office as if they'd been there the whole time. His superior never noticed that his library, too, was expanding. The Guardian took comfort in the fact that the government—personified in the Department Head with his mustache and dour expression—wasn't as smart as he'd thought. And during those heady days, the crabs stopped appearing in his dreams and he became aware of things that he'd always known, things he'd long resisted: The world was a labyrinth and the rabbits would turn up no matter what.

Days went by, weeks perhaps, even months, he wasn't sure. Since that first book, time might as well have been a desert of soft sand. In those days, he was content. He read dozens of books. Some of these he stashed in his wardrobe, warning his wife not to open it under any circumstances. *Leave the ironed clothes in the laundry room*, he told her. He'd put them away himself, as he'd been entrusted with secret files belonging to the Authority and he couldn't betray the confidence of his superiors.

He grew adept at living two lives—one secret, one public—and became so accustomed to this that he wondered if every citizen in the republic had a hidden life. How many people furtively read unadulterated copies of the Holy Books? Chanted ancient hymns and believed in heaven and the afterlife? Kept DVD players and watched science fiction movies? Memorized poetry, then whispered it like an incantation? Or devoured delectable stories like *Little Red Riding Hood*, *Pinocchio*, or *Sinbad the Sailor*? Comfortable with his lying, he found that he was good at it. *If I'd been born in a different time, I probably would have been a writer.*

Only one thing marred his happiness—his daughter. Her symptoms were getting worse, and it had become a familiar sight to see her talking to imaginary creatures as she walked through the house. Last time, he'd heard her muttering, "You fly all the time. I'm tired of flying, I want to walk!" One evening, he tried putting on a documentary that one of the censors at the department had praised, but after a few minutes his

157

eyelids grew heavy and his daughter began to fidget. "Baba, when are you taking me to the old man who tells stories?"

She was right, he thought; the old man knew lots of stories, not just the one about the magic mirror. One time, when the Secretary had forgotten how angry he was at the government, he shared the tale of the magic pot that could drown the world in porridge. Since then, the Guardian had become addicted to his storytelling too.

But his anxiety began to climb when his wife pointed out the change in their daughter's appearance: She was losing weight and had gone strangely pale. When she took the child to the doctor, all the tests came back negative. But, for some reason, she tired quickly and always wanted to lie down with her eyes closed. Once, he revealed his worries to the Secretary: "She's not sick, but there's no life in her. I don't know what to do."

Removing his spectacles, as he always did when he believed that serious matters were at hand, the old man said, "Poor child. Reality is poisoning her blood."

The words lodged heavily in his chest. "She needs to adapt like the rest of us."

"When the world is this abysmal, getting used to it is the worst thing that can happen to you."

"What do you suggest then?" he snapped. "Should I just wait for her to die in my arms?"

The old man shook his head. "Look at what they're doing. Why do you want your daughter to adapt to an artificial reality?"

"Because the alternative is death."

"The alternative is resistance, but you're too busy reading novels," said the old man, swatting him on the head with a rolled-up stack of time-off requests that were awaiting the boss's signature.

"Aren't I risking enough by going to the Labyrinth every night?"

"Sure," said the old man, sitting on the edge of his desk and setting the papers down beside him.

He looks quite sprightly for such an old fossil, the Guardian thought.

"But," the Secretary continued, "we will never bring down the System if all you do is move books from the Labyrinth to the Department Head's library."

"The System can never be defeated."

"Thanks to the likes of you."

"I'm not a hero. All I want to do is read."

The old man murmured, *Until they become conscious they will never rebel, and until after they have rebelled they cannot become conscious.*

The Guardian sighed. The line was from *that* novel. The mere thought of it still made him tremble. This discussion was leading nowhere, and he was getting tired of it. He was worried about his daughter—that was all. "What can I do?" he asked.

"Bring her to me. I'll read her a good story. It'll make her feel better."

"Now you're talking crap."

"You of all people know that I'm not."

He sighed again, unable to meet the old man's gaze. "She asks about you all the time."

"I know, I know. Bring her to me."

THE NEXT DAY, things started off well enough. The Guardian of the Library had given his daughter a bath, dried her with warm white towels, and sprinkled baby powder on her stomach and her back so she wouldn't put any on her head. "Here's the fairy dust you asked for," he said. "Do you like it?"

Without waiting for a response, he continued. "Guess what? We're going to see the old man today; he's got a story for you. I bet you're happy about that!"

She was thrilled. She didn't even object to wearing the khaki uniform after he lied and swore that her princess dress was in the wash. And he let her wear her shiny red shoes. Even if she wandered around the corridors of the Authority in those shoes, he thought, everyone would look at her and see some sort of improvement—the monkey's tail would appear to be at least two handspans shorter, and he would look like a good father. Rather, he'd look like a clever father who was capable of molding his daughter into the right kind of child. She asked him if she could at least wear the butterfly wings over her khaki dress, so he picked up a fountain pen, pulled up her sleeve, and drew a little butterfly on the inside of her arm. "Didn't I tell you?" he said, tugging her sleeve back down again. "They hunt butterflies in that place. This way, you can be one and no one will know."

She smiled. Perhaps he could help her adapt to an imagination-free reality by using imagination! Why hadn't he thought of it before?

They were both content that day. She was hopping around like a rabbit let loose in cabbage-leaf heaven. He called her school and told them she'd be coming in late due to a visit to the dentist. To perfect the lie, he actually made an appointment. After she saw the old man and listened to the story, he'd take her to get her teeth checked. The whole way there, they wondered which story the Secretary would read. "I know," she said dreamily, her eyes roaming over the tiny-windowed apartment complexes. "He's going to read *Pinocchio*."

He didn't ask her how she knew; she would say a rabbit told her, or a swallow or a goldfinch, or a stray cat, or the wolf in the wardrobe, or the grandmother in the stomach of the wolf in the wardrobe.

It had been a long time since the Guardian had seen such a good start to the day, a morning without tears or kicking or pretending to be sick. The best thing was that she'd eaten a hearty breakfast: a boiled egg, a green apple, and cornflakes with milk. He and his wife had looked in disbelief as the girl ate. He wondered if her paleness had really disappeared, or if he just imagined it was gone? She kissed her mother before she left and waved goodbye—a first. It was amazing, he thought, what the promise of a story could do.

When they arrived at the Authority and walked through the corridors, he noticed approving glances on everyone's faces. The receptionist, the security guard, and even the seven censors—all noticed the improvement in his daughter's condition. It wasn't a hopeless case after all; the monkey's tail had been tucked away, just a tiny scruff of fur visible to the eye. "Good for you!" They winked and smiled at him every step of the way; he was a good father, a clever father. He was smiling, too—inside and out—and his daughter was behaving perfectly. She didn't even chase the rabbit that waited for her at the department's door, she merely pointed at it and tugged at her father's finger.

"What's wrong with the little one today?" asked the First Censor.

"Dentist's appointment. Bad tooth. I just came in to fill out the permission form. It won't take long."

The censors nodded.

"No problem," said the First Censor. "Take the whole day off."

This was the Authority's way of rewarding him for doing such an excellent job of raising the monkey. He headed for the storeroom where the Authority kept the forms for all administrative procedures. He would meet the Secretary there, and he'd find out which story he was going to read to his daughter.

On boxes full of banned books, ready to be transferred to the prison camp, he sat with the child and waited.

But the old man didn't come.

Half an hour after the time they were supposed to meet, the Guardian realized that something must have happened. A lump formed in his throat and his palms began to sweat. He had to get out of there before he got caught. Grabbing his fidgety daughter's hand, he led her out of the storeroom. Her good mood was fading; she was grumbling, yawning, rubbing at her eyes. She even tried to dig her heels in. She wasn't ready to leave yet, not without a story. He simply dragged her behind him.

They would have to walk past the Secretary's office. He'd caught a glimpse of him on their way in—he was sure the old man had seen him, and that he'd smiled. What had kept him away? His mind skipped through one horrifying possibility after another. *Anything that can go wrong probably will.*

Tightening his grip on his daughter's fingers, he tried to think of a plausible reason to explain why he was still at the Authority, even though the First Censor had given him permission to leave half an hour ago. *My daughter had to go to the bathroom. She ran off after one of those wretched rabbits.* He would never run out of excuses. But where was the old man? As he drew closer to the Secretary's office, he saw that a group of people, including the seven censors, had gathered around the door.

8

THE SECRETARY was on his knees with his hands in the air, surrounded by burly men in black uniforms.

He'd been caught reading.

In his eagerness to meet the child, he'd lost his sense of caution. The First Censor, on stepping unannounced into his office to submit the censors' weekly report, had heard the unmistakable sound of a book closing. He'd seen the old man's face turn red, the sudden vulnerability in his features: his expression was enough to condemn him. It was a *facecrime* in the first degree. So, without waiting for his boss's permission, the First Censor had done what any good citizen would do and reported the old man to the National Security Department.

Everyone was pleased that somebody had finally decided to put a stop to the Secretary's ongoing violations—he'd managed to avoid punishment and had been merrily roaming the Authority's corridors without a hint of shame. This time, the Department Head wouldn't be able to save him, assuming he didn't get in trouble himself—at best he could be charged with negligence, at worst with being an accomplice.

The Department Head was there, his hands in his pockets. He nodded as he answered the investigator's questions and watched the police officers rifle through drawers, shaking out papers and files. They even upended the plastic container in which the old man kept the cabbage leaves for his rabbits. Astonishingly, it wasn't a novel they found or even a book of philosophy. It was an illustrated children's book called *Pinocchio*—a trivial *thoughtcrime* for such a venerable Cancer.

At some point—the Guardian wasn't sure exactly when—the old man had looked at him and his daughter, giving them a strange, secret smile from under his gray mustache. Keeping his mouth closed, he smiled with his eyes, in a way that only people who loved him would recognize. But the Guardian was afraid that he, too, might be caught in a facecrime, so instead of smiling back, he looked away and watched the protesting rabbits, all of them running around in a panic. The police officers handcuffed the Secretary and ordered him to stand up. An officer told the Department Head that his secretary was under arrest: he would be taken to the State Security Office for investigation, and then he'd be tried. In the coming days, everyone in the department would be summoned for questioning.

With an awkward shrug, the Department Head looked at the Secretary as if in reproach. The old man smiled again, a seemingly metaphorical smile, then began to walk away.

A frail, bespectacled, wrinkled old man whose veins bulged from the paper-thin skin of his arms and handcuffed wrists. He was surrounded by seven police officers and followed by seven censors, a Guardian of the Library, a suspicious-looking child, an imaginary wolf, and a colony of rabbits.

FROM A WOODEN
PUPPET TO A
DONKEY

1

ONE COULD TELL they'd left the city behind and arrived in the suburbs when the houses stopped being square. It was almost as if some areas were still untouched by the hand of the Revolution. Coming out here to the suburbs, he thought, was like going back in time to the Old World. Before architecture was standardized by decree, when chaos was still possible and not just a word in the dictionary.

The windows here were different too. Large, with aluminum frames coated in peeling black paint. Even to his novice eyes, these windows were clearly against regulation: a glass pane of this size overlooking a long strip of empty land could stir up all sorts of maladaptive daydreaming. A group of old houses also caught his attention. Some were built of red bricks, others of white, gray, or sand-yellow stone. He remembered seeing a picture of houses like this once in a history book at school. But that was before history became civics and pictures disappeared from the curriculum; studying history—like literature—evoked unnecessary imagination. The houses looked deserted. Perhaps that was why they were there, he thought. To act as relics, tombstones marking the death of the past. Was anyone behind those staring windows? Had the municipality slapped the homeowners with violations for failing to comply with modern building codes? He'd heard about arrests made at a den of Cancers in one of these "haphazard neighborhoods." But what did they mean by "haphazard"? How could the government allow something haphazard to exist in the first place?

Thinking wasn't good for anyone, he reminded himself; it was best left to the authorities. For the last few months, he'd been trying to teach himself this new skill, the skill of not thinking. To make it less tiresome, he decided to look at it as a form of delegating authority. Truth be told, every time he thought too deeply, it all came back to him: the old man in handcuffs walking between seven police officers, seven censors, and a colony of rabbits. Whenever he remembered something like that, something that he couldn't have imagined—even though he wasn't sure about anything anymore—his thoughts froze. They turned blue and clogged his brain.

Why would anyone open a bookstore in a place like this? he wondered. Even someone like him, who knew nothing about running a business, understood that the idea reeked of foolishness. A bookstore out here in the middle of nowhere, while the city was full of markets, hordes of orbiting shoppers staring open-mouthed and drooling at store windows, counting and recounting the measly sums in their pockets. Real customers, not ghosts.

He used to imagine how he would look in the navy suit of a bookstore inspector. Swanky and refined. It was the uniform he'd always wanted to wear, but today it just felt strange. When the First Censor announced that the boss had transferred him to the inspection department, all he felt was the slight slickness of his palms, the heightened labor of drawing a breath.

After driving past the large-windowed houses, he arrived at what looked like a deserted mall. Cracking open the green inspection folder, he confirmed the address—he was in the right place, but it seemed to exist outside of time. The walls were covered in spray paint, a mash-up of bizarre colors, and . . . He saw it but pretended he hadn't. A person could be arrested just for looking at what had been drawn on the wall: a crab waving its pincers in the air. The opposition movement had chosen the Cancer zodiac sign as their logo.

He didn't understand—wasn't it the government who called them Cancers? Why were they proud of being compared to deadly cells in a healthy body? Although if you really thought about it, weren't cancer cells the only ones that thrived in a dying body? That sounded like one of the old man's thoughts. Actually, most of his thoughts were a chaotic blend of voices from books he'd read, voices of characters for whom it was fitting to think this way, and who had the right to do so because they weren't real. Novels, for the most part, were a celebration of strangeness. But he needed to be ordinary—it was safer. That's what he'd decided to do ever since the Secretary was arrested: be ordinary. Live a normal life out of jail. It was as simple as that.

But why had the government decided to pretend this place, an obvious Cancer den, didn't exist? If a lowly bookstore inspector like him could put two and two together, how could the government have missed it? And how could the resistance announce their location so openly? The Old World was creeping back in through a myriad little crevices.

Armed with the inspection file, he braced himself and climbed out of the car.

Since they'd taken the old man, all his contact with the Labyrinth had been severed. How long ago had that been? It was impossible to tell, though he was well aware that, for readers of books, time took on the characteristics of sand in a desert. But he remembered being afraid. With every knock on the door, every ring of the bell, every time someone called his name, his heart would drop into the pit of his stomach. He'd convince himself that his arrest was imminent and that the old man had confessed under the "Truth Extraction Policies" known to everyone with ties to the opposition.

A long time had passed, what felt like a desert's worth of sand trickling through an hourglass, and no one came for him. The old man had held out! Who'd have thought he had it in him? He'd been too scared to inquire after the Secretary, and he hadn't caught a whiff of gossip about him from the seven censors. It seemed as if everyone had forgotten about the old man, as if he'd never existed. And when a new secretary took his place—a young woman wearing glasses with white frames, starched khaki clothes, her black hair tightly pulled back—he began to suspect that the old man had lived only in his imagination.

And then, a couple of days ago, he dreamed of him. Bent over a piece of wood, carving it, giving it a face. On the wall behind him hung dozens of marvelous clocks featuring multicolored sheep, nests full of twittering birds, dancing puppets, dwarves in a forest, elves hammering the sole of a leather shoe—every kind of clock, all of them telling stories.

"I didn't know you were a clockmaker!" he'd said in the dream.

"Yes, you did," said the old man, peering at him over the top of his glasses.

"How would I know that?"

"You knew you needed time to become a human being in the full sense of the word. You knew that right from the start."

How odd, he thought. He stole a glance at the log the clockmaker cradled in his arms. Suddenly, the piece of wood opened its eyes and screamed. He woke drenched in sweat. What had happened to the old carpenter? Why had he disappeared so completely, leaving no trace of who he really was?

The morning after that dream, something highly unusual happened. The Censor found a letter on his desk: he'd been transferred to the inspection department and given an order—to be carried out immediately—for a distant bookstore, outside the borders of his familiar world. He had gone to his boss's office to find out what was going on. Standing ramrod straight in front of the wonderful library he'd helped to build with his nighttime raids on the Labyrinth, he looked at the Department Head, staring into the man's dark eyes as he remembered the story of the reckless princess and her magic mirror. *Why are the idiots always the ones in charge?*

"Why am I being transferred now, sir?"

But his boss just stared at him, bemused. "Haven't you always wanted to work in the inspection department?"

That was before he'd read a single book. But now he didn't know what he wanted; he just knew he felt sick to his stomach. "Hasn't my work been up to scratch?"

The Department Head waved his hand dismissively. A strained grin returned to his face. "No, we need you in the inspection department. That's all."

It was a trek to the bookstore. He trudged along the wall, encountering more graffiti as he went. Cigarettes puffing smoke that morphed into flowers. Butterflies and laughing skulls. Who had the guts to draw these? He gripped the folder tightly; someone might see him. He decided to make it clear to the world that he was an employee on an official assignment, that he believed in the division of responsibilities. Didn't think. Didn't analyze. Had nothing to do with the Cancers—well, except that he liked to boil crabs and eat them, but he had once felt guilty when he saw one squirming in the pot. Since the old man had been arrested, that was the worst crime against the System he could remember having committed. But when it came to reading . . .

He shook his head. "We all have our bad habits," he muttered. "Some of us smoke, some drink, and others read."

Assuming he was still alive, it would make the old man happy in his prison cell to know that the former Book Censor, who was also the former Guardian of the Library *and* a current Bookstore Inspector, had continued to read. Not as much as before, it was true. He now found his fingertips tingling every time he picked up a banned book. And he had to wait every night until his wife's snores filled the room before sneaking a volume from his wardrobe to read a page or two. Lately, though, his rising palpitations had forced him to limit himself: he read a single paragraph each day, preferably poetry. Something he could savor until the next.

He looked around him. All he could see was a mall in the middle of nowhere, full of deserted stores and uninhabited apartments. How in God's name was he supposed to find a bookstore here? Then, on the wall to his right, an odd drawing caught his eye: a white rabbit with upright ears, wearing a suit jacket and carrying a pocket watch. Next to the rabbit was an arrow pointing to a cramped alley. There was only one thing to do: follow the white rabbit.

2

IN PLAIN SIGHT, at the end of the alley, right around the corner from where the rabbit marked the way, he found the bookstore.

Dusty books with tattered covers were scattered on the sidewalk in front of the store. No one had bothered to pick them up, not even the owner. Some had no covers at all—he itched to acquaint himself with what was inside. But he didn't dare look. Was it a trap? Perhaps the old man had informed on him, and they'd sent him to this bookstore in the hinterland to test him. What if everything was not what it seemed? What if the wall, the crab, the jacketed rabbit with the pocket watch, the bookstore itself were all fake? What if Wonderland was the Republic of Big Brother? He swallowed hard and fought back the burning temptation to grab all the books off the sidewalk and run. But he refused to take the bait. The wooden door at the end of the alley was beckoning.

On the mat thrown askew on the doorstep, the words "Keep Out" were emblazoned. His eyes crinkled at the edges.

This bookseller doesn't seem to want to sell any books! They might as well sell raincoats in the desert. Everything here seemed illogical, but charming in a way that had become familiar to him. He could recognize it now—the enchantment of metaphor. This time though, they weren't in a book, nor in his head, but in every detail of the bookstore, which was so infused with metaphors that he swore he could touch and smell them.

The flowerpots by the door—he noticed that they were full of lettuce leaves and struggled to keep a straight face. Everything about this place seemed deliberate, designed especially for him—particularly the smell. If there really were intelligence agents lying in wait behind the door, if this was all just a trap, then it was the most beautiful trap in the world. It was more a work of art, and he was happy to perish in it, drawn to his doom like a moth to a flame.

As he opened the weather-beaten door, its hinges creaked and tinkling little bells announced his arrival. Trepidation clutched at his chest and he closed his eyes. If he opened them and found himself surrounded by books, his heart might stop. But when he opened his eyes again, he felt he'd had the wind knocked out of him.

The volumes on the shelves had titles like *A Woman's Tears, Your Heart is Mine, Because I Love You*. Not to mention the hundreds of books that wanted to teach people how to succeed, make money, and be happy. Books that were fit for circulation, placed on the shelves fully sanctioned by the law. His stomach lurched as if the floor was giving way under his feet. Where were the books he'd been hoping to discover?

"Welcome, Inspector. I've been waiting for you."

He turned his eyes toward where the voice was coming from. Behind the cashier's desk was a woman. A woman who, he decided, was beautiful, even though by the looks of things she was trying to hide it. Take those ugly glasses for instance. And her hair—she'd have been better off letting it cascade over her shoulders. And undoing her top button. And smiling with her eyes, not just with her lips (which were, admittedly, full). She seemed guileful, a wild woman. That was how he saw her, and she hadn't yet said another word.

"You were waiting for me?"

"Of course."

She disappeared for a second as she reached under the desk, and popped back up with a black folder bursting with papers. "Here you are, sir, these are Circulation Approval Certificates, stamped by the Censorship Authority and signed by the Department Head. Every book on these shelves has been certified fit for circulation. You can check for yourself."

"There's no need," he muttered, grinding his teeth. He'd inspected many of these books himself and approved them. He recognized their covers. Not to mention the familiar wave of nausea that hit him, khaki-colored and topped with a viscous layer of foam.

Everything—unfortunately—was in order. The real trap wasn't one baited with books and set up by the intelligence services, it was being utterly and completely disappointed. A sudden weakness came over his legs; he wanted to sit down and grieve.

Because the Secretary had been arrested.

Because he was lonely.

Because he'd been transferred out of the censorship department.

Because he hadn't visited the Labyrinth in what felt like forever.

And because bookstores were all full of shit.

He decided to make a reckless move. Moving closer to the cashier's desk, he stared into the woman's cold, eerily black eyes. "Do you have a copy of *Pinocchio*?"

She looked down her nose at him. "You must be joking, Inspector! That book is banned."

So, she *was* one of those booksellers who confined themselves to the superficialities.

"You said you were waiting for me."

"I was."

"Why?"

The woman grinned like a Cheshire Cat. "The rabbit told me you were coming."

3

AS SOON AS the words were out of her mouth, the bookseller burst out laughing. "Look at your face!"

He didn't get it. The woman was mocking him, chuckling so hard he could barely understand her: " . . . Really had you there . . . pulling your leg . . . worth it . . . you should see yourself!"

With deliberate movements, she sat down on the edge of the desk, then crossed her legs and lit a cigarette.

"I hate mirrors," he muttered. What a pointless thing to say. Even if he did hate mirrors, why would he say so to this quirky bookseller? He decided to put a stop to these thoughts and asked the only logical question: "Who are you?"

"I'm the bookseller."

"You just said something . . . something about rabbits."

"Calm down." The woman said this as if she no longer found his ignorance entertaining, now that her mirth had subsided. "When it comes to rabbits, there's no need to explain anything."

He hung his head and stared at the floor—a failed student.

"I was under the impression that he'd trained you properly," she said.

"Who?"

"The old carpenter."

"Oh—"

She blew smoke out of her nostrils, her face suddenly tinged with sadness. "What do you think of my bookstore?"

"It's the biggest disappointment of my life."

Laughing again, she ground out her cigarette. "Are you looking for books?"

"I'm a book inspector, it's pretty much my job."

"I have something for you." The bookseller took the Inspector's hand and led him through a door discreetly positioned behind the cashier's desk, leaving behind the enormous file of Circulation Approval Certificates. The touch of her hand made his blood flow hot in his veins. He would have pushed her away, rubbed at his palm until every trace of her was gone, but he didn't want her to see him as he was: boorish and weak. Where was this wild woman taking him? At the back of the store, a string curtain of little bells hung across a doorway into a square concrete room where two armchairs and a mahogany coffee table sat on top of a woven rug. She shifted the table and kicked the rug aside, revealing a trapdoor.

The Inspector peered down the opening. "What's this?" he asked.

"It's the rabbit hole."

I know this place. It was the never-ending tunnel he'd been falling down in his dreams.

"Let's go," said the bookseller, and started down the stairs, practically leaping ahead like one of those goddamn rabbits. Would the walls of this wondrous black hole be lined with books, too? And when the slow descent into the underworld ended, would he find people whose heads grew out of their feet?

The woman was yelling. "Where are you? Hurry up and come on down!"

He wanted to ask, *But what've you got down the—?* Nothing this exciting had ever happened to him, not even in his wildest fantasies. His cheeks were burning, his palms were sweaty—

"Stop being an idiot!" said a voice in his head, and this time he recognized it at once. It was the old man's voice. "You know perfectly well what's waiting for you at the bottom."

It was a winding staircase, just a regular winding staircase. He would go down now, turning around the same point again and again, but moving downwards, always downwards. Well, whether it was Wonderland or the Republic of Big Brother down there, he'd go and find out for himself.

Just like in the dream whose walls were lined with books, it took him a fair amount of time to get down to the basement, particularly since this was not a fall in the strictest sense. Halfway down, he heard the bookseller's voice: she was singing, like a child amusing herself with echoes. And when he eventually got to the end of the staircase—muscles stiff, limbs trembling—he found himself in pitch darkness and thought at once of the bodies that might be buried in this basement, the bodies of all the inspectors who had visited before him.

"Where are you?" he asked. His voice shook slightly, and he hoped she wouldn't notice. Then a switch clicked and everything was made clear. Even though he'd reached the bottom of the staircase, his heart was still in free fall. He stood, leaning against the wall behind him, straining to see the full extent of the wooden shelves that filled every inch of this underworld. A bookstore! A proper one, with the right smell and the right contents too! His fatigue evaporated as he wandered the tall columns of books on either side of him, brushing his hands over their surfaces as if he were petting a cat.

"You look like you're doing well!" he said to the titles, his lips spreading into a grin. It had been a long time since he'd felt so physically close to books, or seen so many of them. And not just any books! Banned books. The right books. Books that stirred up trouble, threatened public order, offended society's morals, and rattled the world's confidence. Books he used to steal from the government's warehouse to save from being burned. Real books with catastrophic influence, equally able to create and destroy.

He stood in front of a tower of old volumes, touching one spine after another, making sure his back was turned to the bookseller in case any inappropriate expression came over his face. It wouldn't do for a man to cry in front of a woman—he was one of those people who believed in this—especially if she was beautiful. But all he really wanted to do was turn back and thank her.

"So?" Her voice came near in a mocking whisper. "What are you going to do, inspector? Arrest me?"

He turned to face the woman. She was lighting another cigarette. "I just have one question."

"What is it?"

"Do you have *Pinocchio*?"

4

"STOP FOOLING AROUND. Don't you get it? You're here for a reason."

It hadn't crossed his mind. Even now—when he was obliged to think about what she'd said—he wasn't interested. It wasn't that he'd slipped back into the convoluted paths of doublethink, but rather that he was enjoying the idea of not analyzing why he was here. Because all he wanted to do was to explore these books. To touch them, smell them, feel the scratch of their rough paper against his thumb. To hear the quaint rustling of turning pages.

He wanted to be their water: Books grew thirsty, too, and demanded their right to be read, so why for the love of God was that woman yammering on?

"You don't have *Pinocchio* here?"

"Don't change the subject," she said sharply.

Does she have to be so harsh?

"You're the Guardian of the Library."

His voice broke. "That was a long time ago."

"You must go back to the Labyrinth."

His fingers froze two inches from a book in front of him and hovered in midair. His eyes traveled to the woman's face, then to the floor. He hadn't been back to that place since the old man's arrest. He didn't think he could go there again. Fear had taken over his life, and he'd spent the last few months training to become invisible, so that even if someone reported him, he'd never be found. But how had this woman found him? "I can't," he mumbled.

She shrugged. "Well, there's no other way."

"It's not that easy."

How had this bookseller managed it? Not just finding him, but getting him transferred to the inspection department and tasked with checking out this particular bookstore. These Cancers always found a way to infiltrate the System. Wonders never cease.

"Listen," she said. "Purification Day is coming up and, according to our sources, they're planning to burn at least ten thousand books. A massacre! You've got to do something about it."

But he had a different bone to pick. "Where've you Cancers been all this time?"

"Waiting."

"For what?"

"For the right time to transfer you to the inspection department."

"What about the Secretary? Is there any news of him?"

The bookseller bit her lip and shook her head.

He sighed. "I can't steal ten thousand books."

"No one's asking you to."

"Well, I don't like your idea of choosing 'worthy' books to save."

"Ah, you must be one of those holdout supporters of the old democratic regime."

She said this as if it amused her, but he didn't find it funny. He wasn't a fan of democracy, and books had nothing to do with it.

"Look, we're talking about rare copies, manuscripts of important books. We can't go on without them." She was getting carried away, her voice wavering. Perhaps the steely, chain-smoking woman wasn't as tough as she looked.

"You sound just like him."

"Who?" she asked.

"The old man."

"He trained me himself."

"I can tell."

Emotion clouded her features and her eyes glimmered with distant memories. "He used to read everything I wrote," she said.

"You're a writer?"

"Sometimes."

"What do you write?"

"None of your business."

"Not the kindest, are we?"

"The sooner you get that into your head, the better. It'll make things easier for both of us."

The woman blew out an exasperated breath. Every time she tried to put him on the right track, he swerved away with another irrelevant, silly question. Talking about the Labyrinth didn't interest him nearly as much as getting to read what she'd written. A writer's manuscript! He'd never even seen such a thing before! What would it look like? His index finger was busy tracing the gilded title stamped onto the thick leather cover of a dictionary. Tired of her insistence, he mumbled, "I can't sneak into the boss's library to hide the books."

"You're meant to bring them to me. Haven't you figured that out yet?"

In all honesty, he preferred to stick to the old routine. Any change would stir up his anxiety. He was no hero—he'd already confessed as much to the Keeper of the Labyrinth—and this role didn't suit him at all: the brave knight offering his services to an iron-willed bookseller, saying, "Your wish is my command." And she wasn't making things any easier.

"What about the raids? What if they come and search this place?"

"That's why *you* were transferred to the inspection department."

"Well, what if a different inspector comes?"

"We'll keep him upstairs, safely on the surface of course, with all the 'good' books. How else do you think we've survived all these years?" She glared at him. "Do I need to explain everything to you?"

He pretended to be engrossed in a copy of *A Thousand and One Nights*. He picked it up, opened it to a page in the middle, and examined the metaphors caught in the fabric of the language.

"So, what do you say?"

"Frankly, I never wanted to become an inspector. At least when I was a censor, I could read at work without worrying about breaking the law. But now . . . "

Now he read in his bedroom, and there were only a handful of books hidden in his wardrobe. He'd read them all several times already, and he was hungry for new words.

"I'm not a Cancer anymore."

"Not a Cancer?"

"No. I have a daughter and I worry for her."

"Well then, get out," said the woman, her face an icy mask of calm. A snow queen. She turned her back on him and hunched over to light yet another cigarette.

How could he leave this place when he could hardly believe he'd found it?

"You know your way out."

"I'm not—"

"If you're not a Cancer, you have no right to be in this part of the store. I'll take you back upstairs. You'll have to arrest me."

"I'm not going to arrest you."

"That means you're a Cancer. Or perhaps you've been infected with doublethink, like all the other *good* citizens. The way I see it, there are only two ways about it: either slap me in handcuffs or help me out."

"And what if I refuse?"

"Then I'll ask you to go upstairs, and I'll suggest a couple of titles for you to read from those books of drivel you love so much."

So his instincts had been spot-on. This bookseller was capable of torture. For a moment, he imagined himself strapped into an electric chair, a book held open in front of his face, sighs rising from its pages like sour fumes, the woman's crazed screams egging him on, *Read! Read more!* And every time he stopped and refused to read another line, she would electrocute him.

"Evil is what you are."

And very clever, he wanted to add, but that would make her even harder to deal with. He felt like a wooden doll, controlled by invisible strings that stretched out from the woman's hands. She was the unseen puppet master, a writer dictating the fate of one of her characters. He wondered if she wrote novels, and if he would ever read a book she'd written. Perhaps he might get the chance when she stripped off her armor and spoke in gentler words, ones without claws.

"Fine. I'll go to the Labyrinth."

"Good."

"*Now* can I buy a copy of *Pinocchio*?"

5

ONCE AGAIN, the former Book Censor and current Inspector became a Guardian of the Library. Just like in the old days, he stole into the Labyrinth at every opportunity. He met the strange caretaker, lost his way, read for a while, and grew even more lost. Then, remembering the old man, he'd steal the chosen books for the bookseller's basement of contraband.

On his first visit to the Labyrinth after the long, painful estrangement, he'd found the Keeper of the Labyrinth waiting for him as if nothing had happened. The same shirt and that same headcloth. Bare feet, beefy forearms, and sunburned skin. "Hey, Boss! Brother! Where've you been?"

He knew that the resistance always hacked the security system at a specific time of the day, when one of its operatives was stationed at the surveillance camera, tasked with erasing the recordings. He had to be there at the right time when the system was compromised. According to the bookseller, it had been much easier to infiltrate systems in the past, using computers. But with the rationing of technology and all the other changes that came after the Revolution, thieves, pirates, and contraband smugglers like them had to do everything in person, not through glowing screens. Apart from that, lawbreaking went on as it always had.

As the days went by, he was cured of fear and began to enjoy breaking the law, slipping through its loopholes. And yet he was still terribly lonely. Even though he read hundreds of pages every day, he had no one to talk to. But he found some solace in visiting the bookseller.

Sometimes—ignoring the doormat's instructions to "Keep Out"—he'd stride into the bookstore, announced by little bells, and see her set aside a pen and squirrel papers away in a drawer. In the few seconds it took for him to walk over to the cashier's desk, the incriminating evidence was gone. It was out of the question that she'd write while he was there, let alone allow him to see what she'd written. It crossed his mind that she might have fallen in love with him. Perhaps he inhabited her thoughts night and day as she wrote fiery poems about him—most likely full of cursing and swearing. But her cold greetings quickly put to bed any such possibility. No doubt she forgot about him as soon as he left, only remembering him the instant he returned.

Once, he'd been bold enough to ask, "When do I get to read what you've been writing?"

"You don't want to read what I write," she said with a dismissive wave, as if swatting away a pesky fly.

"Why not?"

"You won't like it. Simple as that."

It occurred to him that she might be suffering from that common malady of writers—a lack of self-confidence. He took this as a sign that she might in fact be writing real literature.

"I've never read a manuscript before."

"It's not that simple."

"Please."

"Why?"

"I want to have a hand in the process." How he longed to step into the writing kitchen, to roll up his sleeves and get elbow-deep in ink. He wanted to lie on his back under the great machine of literature, inspect the nuts and bolts, take apart the secret code behind the magic. All the books he'd read so far were finished products; they didn't need his input. Why not read a working manuscript? But the woman shifted her eyes away and blushed, making him wonder again if she was infatuated with him.

"You don't know what you're talking about." That's what she usually said by way of changing the subject. This time, when his persistence grew tiresome, she decided the visit had come to an end, opened the door, and set the little bells jangling. "Go home to your wife."

The Guardian never came across a single customer at the bookstore, and he had no idea how the bookseller paid her rent. He wondered if the "Keep Out" sign on the doormat was actually discouraging people, but the woman laughed at this suggestion and told him the sign was there to attract readers because they weren't very good at following orders.

"Does that mean there are readers out there who know about your bookstore? Why haven't I met any of them?"

"Readers as a species are nearly extinct," she said. "What did you expect?"

With a business that was losing so much money, he suspected she didn't have a place of her own. He could see her, after each long day's work, like a goddess of the underworld, heading down to that dark basement filled with forbidden books and falling asleep on the floor, a book cradled in her arms. He reckoned that if she'd take off her glasses, get rid of her hideous hairdo, and get a good night's sleep, she wouldn't look so fierce. But that didn't answer his question. *How does she pay her bills? Where does she get the money to live on if I'm her only customer and get all my books for free?*

Once, as they sat on the dusty floor in the basement of forbidden titles, telling each other what they'd read the night before, he realized that she was about a million books ahead of him. Every time the bookseller opened her mouth to talk about another book she'd read, he felt diminished. It had been easier to swallow when he'd been the Secretary's disciple—after all, the old man was ancient. But when it came to this woman, deep down, he wished she was faking it.

The bookseller had told him that she came from a long line of "book people." That her ancestors were all poets, writers, and booksellers. Her great-grandfather could read books—and even buy and sell them—on a small, lit-up screen, but he preferred books he could touch.

"My grandfather once wrote that the idea of losing the books stored in the cloud worried him more than a possible fire in his bookstore," she told him. Her gaze anxiously skimmed the books on her shelves like a protective mother. "And he was right. After the Revolution, hundreds and thousands of books that were published on the internet were lost forever, even though some people insist they're still somewhere in the cloud."

The Guardian found it baffling: what did clouds have to do with glowing screens? Unless, of course, people used to speak in metaphors back then. That reminded him of the early days when he'd just started out as a guardian of surfaces.

"I never believed that language was a smooth surface," he said once, out of the blue. He was hoping to impress her.

The woman raised an eyebrow. "Didn't you?"

"They keep saying we must only skim the surface of language. But language is not just a smooth surface. The System is wrong."

He thought himself very brave in spelling it out. *The System is wrong.* If the old man had been there, he'd have given him a proud pat on the head because he'd never said anything of the sort out loud before. An inexplicable happiness filled his chest; he hoped the bookseller would gaze at him like a princess at a knight who'd just slayed a dragon. Instead, she leaned forward to light a cigarette, blowing smoke from her nostrils as she gave him a searching look. She looked more like a dragon.

"But the System's right," she said.

He was thunderstruck. "What do you mean?"

"All language is a surface, and what lies beneath, on the bottom, is more of a rippled riverbed—made so by the force of a poem, for example." She went quiet for a moment before continuing: "The most ridiculous war you can ever wage is the war of one metaphor against another."

The Guardian had never felt so small. A lonely Don Quixote with a broken lance, guarding surfaces from the encroachment of language. And she was belittling him, disparaging every experience he'd been through. *Is she picking on me on purpose?* he thought. *Or is she just living in her own head, trying out one idea and knocking down another, in a never-ending game that—to her—is life itself?*

This had happened frequently in the past few days. She'd say something like, "The bottom is a furrowed surface," or some other such crap from the System, and he would feel—besides disappointment—that he hated this woman. She was a hateful impostor, with a predilection for making false arguments. But beside her, every other person's company tasted like boiled cauliflower.

6

THAT AFTERNOON, when the Guardian went to pick up his daughter from school, she wasn't there.

She wasn't in the schoolyard with the other children as usual. Had she gotten into trouble again? She was probably still sitting in the naughty chair in class. That had happened before, at least twice. "There's no need to worry," he muttered to himself. He darted across the back garden, past the rabbit hutch, through the porcelain-tiled corridors. Without thinking, he stepped on the grass, ignoring the Keep Off sign. His heart pounded—had he really just broken the rules in broad daylight?

When he reached the classroom, he saw that his daughter wasn't there either. As he poked his head around the half-open door, he realized what he knew would now be obvious to the teacher—he was already showing nearly all the symptoms common to parents in the first minutes after their children disappear: a strange trembling in the fingertips, little drops of sweat dripping from the pores of the nose, unusually pale lips that looked as though they'd been outlined with a white pen. But he hadn't—yet—reached the point of screaming and smashing things up.

The teacher calmly walked toward him, gliding eerily over the floor without seeming to touch it. He couldn't hear her footsteps at all. *Footsteps? Of all the things to be thinking about at a time like this!* Pain hit him like a ton of bricks; he felt as if his organs were being crushed, almost snuffing the very life out of him. He watched the teacher draw closer. *Why isn't she looking at me?* Her eyes were fixed on the floor, her lips clamped as if she were holding a pebble between them that was about to drop. The Guardian knew what it meant when people behaved this way. His stomach clenched. "Where's my daughter?" he asked.

"The principal is waiting for you in her office."

Was that an apologetic note in her voice? In any case, she didn't make eye contact, staring instead at his forehead. He looked at the naughty chair in the corner of the classroom, unwilling to believe it was empty.

Cursing, he headed for the principal's office at a fast trot, hoping his daughter had simply gotten into a fight with another child, and that all he'd have to do would be to tell her to apologize. He went back through the corridors, across the back garden, past the rabbit hutch to the administration office. Dozens of doors. Even more walls. In every room, there was someone who led him somewhere else—he couldn't make heads or tails of the place. When he finally arrived at the principal's office, his daughter wasn't sitting in any of the chairs along the wall with the other wayward children. That's when it sunk in.

"Where is she?"

"Please sit down."

"Where's my daughter?"

The principal pointed to a chair, but he refused to sit. He stood there glaring at her, feeling no need to disguise his hatred, waiting for her to tell him what he already knew.

"*Where* is she?"

She swallowed. This woman wasn't looking him in the eye either. He wondered if they'd all been instructed to act this way.

"There was a school inspection today. They came in to assess the second-year students' readiness to advance through elementary school, and your daughter—"

"What about her?"

"I think you can guess what happened."

"Did she fail the exam?"

"They transferred her and one other girl to the rehabilitation center." She held out a slip of paper. "This is your summons to report to the center."

His eyebrows shot up. "Am I under investigation?"

They take my daughter and then act as if I'm the criminal!

Still avoiding his eyes, the principal launched into a speech that was clearly rehearsed. "It's routine procedure. The parents of all children showing symptoms of imagination are investigated to see if they've fulfilled their child-rearing obligations. Actually, parents usually leave the centers pretty quickly. Everyone knows it's a complicated matter: A family can do everything right, and the child might still grow up suffering from imagination. It happens—sometimes it comes down to biological reasons."

A strange humming filled his head. *What shit is this old hag spewing?*

"Can I see my daughter?"

"That's up to the specialists at the center."

Of course. He knew that already. At the center, they might arrest him, detain him for questioning, or kick him out into the street. Whatever happened, he wouldn't see his daughter until she'd been through a long period of treatment. He couldn't see her until the government allowed him to do so. Everything—ultimately—belonged to the government. There was no guarantee that he would see his child again. The doctors might decide that seeing him might make her relapse. The truth that no one ever admitted was that children who went into rehabilitation centers sometimes lost their minds, or their lives. But they never lost their imagination.

7

NEITHER THE GUARDIAN of the Library nor his wife had ever visited a rehabilitation center before, but they remembered—knew by heart, even—all the pictures and information from the awareness campaigns that encouraged parents to visit the nearest center if their children showed Old World symptoms. They were just like the campaigns that recommended getting vaccinations on time or visiting clinics for incontinence.

In the advertisements, rehabilitation centers looked like pleasant places with pretty young nurses—that's what every child who is different needs, right? To be cared for by a wide-eyed girl with a perfect set of teeth and a small nose. The ads showed children smiling, singing patriotic songs, doing their early-morning exercises, and attending intensive classes—personalized for each child's case—to straighten their lopsided thoughts. But the last scene in the trailer, the scene that really worried him, featured a little boy waving at the camera a few moments before a black helmet with blue, red, and gray wires protruding from the top of it was placed on his head. It was the government's latest brainwashing invention.

The devices were meant to kill the brain's centers of imagination, to stimulate centers of logic instead—a child couldn't have both. What nobody said was that the results were weak and the side effects were extremely dangerous. A child could lose his memory, for example, or his ability to speak. Most often, children would no longer be able to call things by their names; he'd heard dozens of stories about children who called trees "candlesticks," and described houses as "snail shells."

Before he was arrested, the old man had told him about cases like this, where the government had opted to send a child to Room 101, otherwise known as the Room of No Return—these children could not be let out into the world calling things by the wrong names. According to the old man, when children were unable to speak in anything but metaphors, they were not considered treatable, and had to be dealt with. The government would never allow rumors to spread that questioned the effectiveness of its treatment policies. It was always easier to tell parents that their child had passed away midtreatment than to simply admit that the treatment had failed.

Only the highest members of government and a few Cancers knew about Room 101.

The ads showed gardens and swings and perfect khaki-clad children, busy with Scouting activities, even chanting "Long live the Revolution," as if the whole thing hadn't been settled a long time ago. This was how Big Brother's republic looked when it grew old. No security forces patrolled the streets. If you were arrested for reading a banned novel, hardly anyone would care. The System had taken possession of everything, and it knew that it had won, but it still felt threatened by a child's imagination.

The Guardian stopped his car in one of the parking lots near the pyramid-shaped structure with flat, windowless, brown surfaces. His wife, who'd been sitting teary-eyed in the passenger seat, trembled when she saw the building. "This doesn't look right," she said.

She'd been hoping to see her daughter through a glass window, chasing pigeons in a big garden full of other children. The Guardian couldn't find any words. The silence turned to stone in his gullet, scratching and scraping his throat. "Let's go," he finally said.

His wife began to weep. "This place is horrible! Horrible! Why didn't they take her to a different center, like the ones in the ads?"

"Nothing in real life looks like the ads."

She looked at him, panicked, her eyes wide with terror. "Stop talking like that!" she said. "This is all your fault. We should have told the doctor when we first noticed it. It would have made things easier, at least they would've let us see her. But you refused. All you did was say no!" She buried her face in her hands, sobbing.

"Our daughter is not sick."

"You and your stories and your books in the wardrobe. Did you think I hadn't noticed? You poisoned my daughter's mind. I'll never forgive you. Never!"

Unable to bear any more, he got out of the car, leaving his wife to follow. His wife who would never forgive him. But would she turn him in?

He gave his ID to the security guards at the entrance and showed them the summons. "I'm here about my daughter."

"Wait here until the investigating officer comes for you."

The place looked more like a police station than a hospital. He sat down. His wife sat two chairs away. He wanted to reach for her hand but couldn't. He must weather his fear all alone. *What if she's right? What if I caused this?* He looked around. There were other families waiting, with the same terror in their expressions. Fellow victims of the latest inspection campaign. More children implicated by their vivid imaginations. Monkeys from the Old World with giant, impossible-to-ignore tails.

A few minutes later, two officers arrived. One of them took his wife into room three, and the other took him into room four. *This really is an interrogation*, he thought. He looked on as his wife followed the officer, her head low, willing her to turn back before the door closed. He'd be able to tell from her eyes whether she was going to rat him out. She never met his eyes.

He sat across the desk from the investigator. In this city, nearly everyone dressed in khaki except for the police, who wore black. The worst thing was their gloves, black gloves that looked like the fists of death. *Why black? So they wouldn't be too hard to wash if they were stained with a little . . .* He swallowed and looked at the man's handsome face, his thick mustache, broad shoulders, brown eyes, and dreadful grimace. In another life, he worked for a man who resembled this one, looked just like him in fact. He wondered if they were related.

"What have you done with my daughter?"

8

"WE ASK the questions here."

The investigator opened the file in front of him and wrote down the date and the father's name. There was a field on the left side of the form where the officer made mysterious notes. The Guardian had the most visceral feeling that he was a book, and the investigator a book censor.

"When did you first notice your daughter showing signs of mental deficiency?"

Without taking his eyes off the man, without blinking, he clutched the arms of the chair. "I never noticed anything of the sort." He wondered if his nose was growing a little longer, but his face didn't feel any different.

"It would be better for you and for the child if you cooperate."

"I am."

"I'll repeat the question: When did you notice your daughter showing signs of being different?"

"What kind of signs are we talking about?"

Grumbling, the officer took a piece of paper from the drawer and waved it in his face. "This is the medical report. Shall I read it to you?"

He shrugged.

The officer blew out an irritated breath. Apparently he wasn't used to investigations in which people dared to express dissent. He fixed his eyes on the paper and read: "Hallucinations; Low levels of loyalty to the nation; Imaginary friends; Illegal knowledge of banned stories; Failing to adhere to the national uniform; Detachment from reality; Possession of a forbidden book. Conclusion: Unsuitable for elementary education. Requires complete reprogramming of the brain. Severity: Nine out of ten." The investigator stopped reading and shot him a sideways look. "Do you know why they stop at nine out of ten?"

"No. Why?" He couldn't take his eyes off the investigator's black gloves.

"Because a severity of ten means the child is dead."

The Guardian flinched. *No, I'm not afraid. I'm furious, that's all. So angry I could smash the officer's skull, blow up this building, and murder the seven censors.* He struggled to control himself and keep calm. "That report means nothing. A bunch of over-blown fluff. All children suffer from imagination, it's a vestige from the Old World. And I know about these things—I used to be a book censor. Such symptoms disappear by themselves with the help of elementary education, as we all know. Isn't that what schools are for?"

"Not for an advanced case like your daughter's."

"Let's be rational about this. We all have meaningless vestiges: the appendix, the tailbone, the residues of imagination. They're nothing. Insignificant." As he spouted these words he'd learned by heart, parroting what the government said, he asked himself, again, whether his nose had grown.

The officer put the paper down on the desk, pulled off his gloves, and cracked his knuckles. "What about the book she had with her?"

"I'm an inspector. If I find a banned book, I confiscate it and it stays in my car for a day or two until I visit the Authority building and hand it over to the people in charge. She's just a little girl—she probably found it and took it to school. What was the book anyway?"

"Let's see . . . " the officer muttered, struggling to read the title. "*Pee-no-chee-o*."

This twist in the investigation made him feel like *he* was a goddamned puppet. Nothing but a stupid piece of wood who, instead of becoming a real boy, had turned into a donkey and ruined everything. It was the book the bookseller had given him. The one he'd been so desperate to get. His daughter had taken it to school with her and gotten herself caught. And now he was all alone, and the Secretary was far away, too far to be able to help, trapped in the cavernous belly of the state security prison. The old man's face haunted him. The carpenter-clockmaker who sells time so we can become human beings again. *But we don't. We remain donkeys until the end*. He wanted to cry.

The investigator noticed his stricken face. "So you know the book, then."

"Of course I know the book. I want to see my daughter."

"Look. I've been listening to your excuses, and you need to know that *you*—with the flimsy justifications you've been making—have made her condition worse."

"I want to know why the real rehabilitation centers don't look like the ones we see in the ads. This place has no windows, no garden—"

"It's the new vision. Reeducating children to deal with reality."

"Is that so?"

"It is."

"So why don't we see this reality in the ads? Why don't you show us the truth?"

"What do you mean?"

"I mean, what your ads show is completely imaginary, just like any banned novel."

"And does the esteemed censor read many novels?"

"It was my job."

"What about your daughter?"

"What about her?"

"Do you read her bedtime stories?"

His limbs went stiff. "I don't—"

"How did the child know about the old stories?"

"What old stories?"

"Let's see." The officer brought the file up to his face and began to read: "*Peter Pan, The Princess and the Pea, Little Red Riding Hood, The Wonderful Wizard of Oz, Sinbad the Sailor*. Where did she find out about these forbidden books?"

The Guardian smiled. He felt no elongation of his nose whatsoever as he said, "I'm not the one who read her those stories."

"It must be the imaginary rabbit she's always talking about, then," said the investigator, raising an eyebrow.

"No."

"Who then? The wolf in the wardrobe?"

"She just knows them. Made them up in her head, probably."

"What kind of excuse is that?"

"It's called collective memory. For countless years, those stories have lived on in the memories of millions of children. It'll take a lot more than burning books to get rid of them. When the imagination's every outlet is blocked, it will swell up. Occupy reality. Just like your advertisement."

The officer smiled. "I'm afraid you don't quite understand."

"There's nothing *to* understand."

"Listen carefully. You're being charged with parental negligence. You're responsible for your child's mental deficiency, or—at best—you didn't report her condition right away. You will appear before the family court. A judge will decide on an appropriate punishment. You might want to think about getting a lawyer. I'm releasing you now, but you can be summoned for investigation at any time. Your house, your car, and your place of work are all considered crime scenes, and will be inspected regularly to make sure the home environment is free of thought toxins."

"I want to see my daughter."

"She's not your daughter anymore. Her guardianship has been assigned to the government. She'll be referred to the labs for more tests and a tailored treatment plan. The matter of returning her to your custody depends on the court ruling and on how well she responds to treatment, which will become clear over the next six months."

The Guardian fixed his eyes on the officer's face. He was no longer angry, he was broken. "I need to see her. *Please.*" There were tears in his eyes. He understood things as they were. No one could go up against the System. No one came out of the whale's belly alive.

The officer blew out a breath. For a fleeting moment, he looked sorry for the Guardian. "Fill out a visit request form, put in convincing reasons, and the committee will decide on it."

"What if the committee doesn't approve? What if I never see her again?"

The officer sighed. "Look. It might be too early for this, but we almost always advise parents to move on with their lives. Have other children. And considering your daughter's case . . . Just bear it in mind."

9

ON THE DRIVE HOME, he was completely silent.

He didn't say a word to his wife. It was pointless. If she'd ratted him out, he would have been behind bars by now, but he was free and his daughter was locked up. He might never see her again, his little girl with baby powder sprinkled on her head. He believed it all now. The baby powder was indeed fairy dust, and there really was a wolf in the wardrobe with a grandma in its belly who tasted delicious because she knew so many stories. These details cut him like tiny blades.

His wife leaned her head against the window, sobbing as if their daughter were already dead. Only death wouldn't be the worst thing that happened to her. She'd have to go through intensive brainwashing, and if she ever made it out of that place alive, she would have forgotten him and her mother, the rabbits and the wolf in the wardrobe too. When she got out—if she got out—she wouldn't be his daughter. And when that moment came, they would continue to sneak into her dreams at night, plant microchips in her brain, and surround her with screens spewing out their messages in sound and video. They'd do everything it took to transform her into a model citizen. *Fuck the government!* Tears welled up in his eyes and he ground his teeth, tightening his grip on the steering wheel as if he might snap it in two.

His daughter would end up crying all the time. She'd be alone and they certainly wouldn't let her have a stuffed wolf to cuddle in bed. All she'd see in the coming days would be sterile laboratories, black and red wires, and the President's projected face. Poked and prodded, her blood, urine, and saliva taken for testing. And all around her there would be doctors, psychologists, and soldiers. Loyal citizens serving their country. *Screw the country!*

His little girl would call out for her parents again and again. Kicking and screaming every time the screens showed the President's face. It might take weeks before she realized no one would save her. And only then, perhaps, she'd forget who she was and become what they wanted her to be.

A tear rolled down his cheek. He rubbed his face on his shoulder; he didn't want to cry in front of his wife, but he was broken. He didn't want another daughter. Didn't want one of those government-approved children. Children without imagination. Without stories. Without imaginary friends. A wave of longing tore at him. He was the father of the most wonderful daughter in the world, a child made of metaphors, like a character escaped from a picture book. And now they wanted to ruin her. No one would believe all those things he'd said in the investigation, even though they were true. Nobody believed the truth these days; two plus two didn't make four, and never would, not unless the government wanted it to. But at least *he* understood the truth of what he'd said. He hadn't read those stories to his daughter. She simply knew them. She was both narrator and narrated-to. There was no need for her to invent anything, the stories simply flowed out of her, remembered from a past she hadn't lived.

And he'd said what he said—not in the old man's voice, nor Zorba's or Alice's or even Pinocchio's. Everything he'd said had been in his own voice, but their words were still there, distilled into his.

"What are we going to do?" His wife's voice cracked, marred by sobs.

He remained silent, not because he had no words to offer but because he didn't want to scare her even more. He'd made up his mind; he would call on the resistance for help. The System was compromised, he knew that now. He himself had outmaneuvered it dozens of times. He'd stolen the books and no one had suspected him. Surely the resistance could do the same for a child. There must be someone who could help him. But until that happened, he had to get rid of the contraband he had in his possession.

He parked in front of the house and rushed inside, heading straight for his bedroom. Flinging the wardrobe doors open, he stuffed the books hidden behind his hanging shirts into bags and boxes. He would clear up the crime scene completely, and they could search his house to their hearts' content. Grabbing his wife's car keys, he slunk out the back door, looking around furtively. He heard his wife scream after him, "Where are you going?" But he couldn't afford a single second to console her. The battle had begun.

"We're all wooden puppets here," he muttered before starting the car and taking off.

HOTTER THAN 451
FAHRENHEIT

1

"HELP ME!"

The Guardian of the Library called out to the bookseller as he nudged the door open with his foot, lugging a box of banned books from his wardrobe. Damp stains spread under his armpits. Crying had left his eyes bloodshot and dry as stone.

The woman—as was her habit—had been busy writing something on a sheet of paper. But as soon as she looked up, her face changed. She rushed to help him with the books, throwing a quick glance into the street to make sure he hadn't been followed. "What on earth happened to you?" she asked.

He didn't answer, unable to speak. Leaving the box on the floor in front of the entrance, he went back to his car and returned with a paper bag. Meanwhile, the woman dragged the heavy box behind the cashier's desk, where it could remain hidden until she moved it into the basement. When the man appeared again with the last of the books, she flipped the sign on the door to "Closed" and turned the lock twice. The tinkling bells sounded strange to his ears, like chimes from another world, another life that had ended long ago.

"Are you being watched?"

The possibility hadn't crossed his mind, even though the investigator had told him that his house, his car, anything he touched would become a crime scene. Every inch would be searched. He felt cursed, like the king in one of the old man's stories whose touch turned everything to gold—including, by accident, his royal daughter. Had there been enough time for them to follow him? He hadn't noticed anyone. He wanted to believe he still had one more hour before descending into another circle of hell.

He sat on the box he'd brought in. His voice trembled and broke. "They took my daughter," he said. His eyes welled again, and the woman looked away.

The ironhearted bookseller couldn't stand the sight of tears. "Pull yourself together," she said.

"Help me."

But she refused to meet his gaze, as if his miserable condition was infectious. She poured him a glass of water from the bottle on the desk. He gulped it down.

"Let's go downstairs," said the woman, heading to the basement.

One can't talk about the government without venturing beneath the surface. He followed her, wondering if this resilient creature could give him strength. The rabbit's hole swallowed them, the spiral staircase leading to some uncertain place in the underworld.

They sat cross-legged among the books on the floor. Feeling his pulse grow steady, the Guardian told the bookseller what had happened. It all came out—the school inspection, the illicit book, the rehabilitation center, his session with the investigator, the court date, the expected searches of his house. Everything!

He wiped his eyes with his sleeve and fixed her with an imploring look. "I have to see my daughter."

The bookseller took her time to answer. "What makes you think we can do anything?"

"The System is compromised; we get around it all the time. That's the whole point of the Cancers."

"But our influence only goes so far."

"Only because all our efforts go into rescuing books. We'd be better off trying to save our children . . . "

The bookseller was looking at the floor. "Forgive me," she muttered.

He didn't understand why she was apologizing.

"If we had the power to save people, the old carpenter would be out of prison by now."

"What about my daughter?"

"I'm so sorry."

"Stop apologizing!"

She hung her head even lower, accepting the questions he screamed at her without complaint.

"Why are we saving all these books? Who's going to read them if we abandon our children in that hellhole?"

"It's horrible, I know."

"What do you know? Nothing! Do you even know about Room 101? Did the old man tell you his little stories? Didn't *you* learn anything?"

The woman rose and stroked the book spines on the shelf in front of her, like a lonely old woman fussing over her cats. "I'm sorry."

"Enough with the apologizing! Say something real!"

She let out a long breath. Tears pooled in her eyes. This time, she forced herself to look at him. "The government has been kidnapping children from my own family for decades. They put them in those centers and then . . . nothing. No one knows what becomes of them. It's happened so many times—my brothers, my cousins, my friends have lost kids. I blame them all for bringing children into this world when we're unable to protect them. Every day, we take the risk of hacking the Censorship Authority's systems to rescue the books, the research, just so we can save our collective memory. Salvage some sort of idea about what we were before. But we've never been strong enough to save a child, to save the future. For that—and for many other reasons—I'm sorry."

The bookseller's voice wavered on the last of her words. Her tears made his blood pound in his ears. It would have been better if she'd kicked him out of her store like a beggar.

Everything she said boiled down to a single fact: His daughter was lost to him forever.

"You're worse than the government," he spat. He got up and climbed the stairs without another glance, returning once again to the superficialities of the world above.

2

THE MAN no longer knew how many days it had been since his daughter was locked away. He had become a different person—time meant nothing. The clockmaker had disappeared from his dreams. He no longer wanted to buy himself time; he wanted to stop time passing altogether. Time was hellish, and his wife was about to lose her mind. She was constantly washing dishes, rubbing at her fingers, and roaming the house in search of their daughter's belongings—items she herself had burned. Princess costumes, red shoes, the stuffed wolf, even the bottle of baby powder. Everything that might be transformed, by the power of metaphor, into a smoking gun.

"We have to pass the first inspection," his wife said as she tried to sanitize every surface of their house. But the government's sentries would easily find a way to brand him a traitor. At the end of the day, everything belonged to them: meaning, truth, and his daughter.

BEWARE OF BECOMING ENTANGLED IN MEANING! The warning flashed in his mind. It was the first thing they'd said to him at his training as a new censor. But he no longer found it interesting to think about meaning: words had been stripped of what they normally carried. The only thing he wanted was to see his daughter.

Supposedly, sentries would arrive at any moment to search his car and house, including his daughter's bedroom and his own wardrobe, newly emptied of books. But what if they didn't come? What if they didn't have to, because they already knew everything? Like the Supreme up above, who didn't need to come down to see if His creatures were behaving.

He sat, upright and wooden, on the living room couch. The screen in front of him played a documentary about the Revolution. It was one of those shows that normally put him to sleep in under a minute. But today, he stared at the screen as if his life depended on it. If the government was watching from the sky, then there he was, proving that he had repented and was now worthy.

He scanned his surroundings. His house had to look just as it would if it belonged to any other citizen: one who used electricity sparingly and didn't own a dishwasher. Someone who watched all the Revolution's programs and attached himself firmly—with a thousand nails—to its superficialities.

The doorbell rang and he felt his chest tighten. "Have they arrived?"

His wife peered out from behind the curtain. "No, it's the lawyer," she croaked. She was just as nervous, her eyes swollen and dry. Fixing her clothes—khaki skirt, beige shirt—she went to open the door. He stayed where he was, a sad sphinx.

The lawyer came in carrying a leather briefcase stuffed with papers, his black robe folded over one arm. After a quick handshake, he sat down in the seat across from the couch, cast a probing eye around, but made no comment. The wife's cleaning efforts had left everything spotless.

Before the lawyer could open his mouth, the man jumped in to ask the question that had been nagging at him: "Over the course of your career, how many children have you managed to free from the rehabilitation centers?"

The lawyer sighed and rubbed the bridge of his nose. "Not many."

"How many?"

"Three."

He'd been told that this lawyer was the best in the country. Rescuing even one child from the clutches of those centers was, in itself, a miracle.

"What are my daughter's chances of getting out?"

"Not good." The lawyer took a file out of his leather brief-case. "The Public Prosecutor's office is working with the National Intelligence Agency and the Censorship Authority to investigate you. Their suspicions don't stop at parental negligence anymore. In their eyes, you suffer from an obvious decline in patriotic feeling along with Cancerous tendencies in the second degree. Witness statements place you in long meetings with a traitor who compromised the Censorship

Department—a secretary who's currently in prison. And they have proof that you once took your daughter to meet him. Also, a security guard saw you walking out of the building carrying boxes. Since you were hired, many books have gone missing from the storerooms."

He felt an unsettling churning in his stomach. "I work in the book-banning business. Am I supposed to stay away from the materials I've been assigned to inspect?"

"Why were you reading in the storerooms?"

"The other censors are always chatting, and I need peace and quiet."

"But you were reading books other than the ones assigned to you."

A warm red flush spread over his cheeks. His wife's hand reached out for his own, and he laced his fingers with hers. He knew she blamed him, perhaps even hated him, but she was there, enduring the impossible alongside him. He hung his head, unable to believe he'd fallen so far.

The lawyer went on. "And what about that traitor of a secretary?"

"I was as surprised as everyone else. I thought he'd given up reading."

"You were naive enough to leave your daughter in his care?"

His wife pulled her hand away. He stared at the floor. "I had to get a report done that day. The old man was the only one who had time to look after her."

"What about the claim you made, saying you left her in the children's books department?"

"It wasn't possible for me to do that."

"Why not?"

He hesitated.

"I need to have all the facts," the lawyer reminded him.

"Because of the President's picture. She's afraid of it. Children's books these days . . . "

The lawyer nodded. He didn't need any more explanation. "Isn't it odd that the book they found with your daughter is the same one that got the Secretary arrested?"

"It's a rotten coincidence." He felt his nose getting longer, dividing into branches, growing leaves, sprouting nests, landed on by crows . . . Caught unawares.

"And your records at the Authority show that you've only banned one book. A book called—"

"*Zorba the Greek.*"

"Yes."

"That's because they always assigned me books that were perfectly fit for public consumption!"

"Since you began working in inspections, have you reported forbidden books in any of the bookstores you've visited?"

He avoided the lawyer's eyes, defeated on every front. The lawyer pursed his lips.

His wife spoke up. "Maybe you should concentrate on the fact that the child's condition doesn't warrant her being detained, instead of focusing on how suitable the family's parenting is."

"They're two faces of the same coin. To tell you the truth, her condition was deemed a nine out of ten in the medical report. That doesn't bode well."

"W-what do we do?" Her voice was weak and her words tumbled out like a pile of disconnected letters. The Guardian tried to put a hand on his wife's shoulder, but she pushed him away, breaking into angry tears. "Don't touch me!" She told him that she hated him now. Hated him and pitied him.

The lawyer stepped in. "What we can do, at this stage, is make improvements to your personal file. Even if the court gives no weight to parental negligence, it won't tolerate the decline in patriotism." He put his papers back in the briefcase, preparing to leave.

"What am I supposed to do?"

"Prove your loyalty."

"And how do I do that?"

The lawyer dusted off his trousers, staring at him as if he couldn't believe he had to explain something so obvious. "Do what everyone else does," he said, then got up and made his way out, the little girl's parents trailing after him.

At the door, the lawyer turned back, his face grim. "The first hearing is in two weeks. You'd better leave the prosecutor's questions to me, since you clearly have a death wish."

"I WANT TO REPORT a bookstore for selling banned books."

He announced this to the Department Head, hoping even then for some kind of reward—a pat on the shoulder, a grin—but the Department Head seemed completely taken aback. He even challenged him with a hushed, "Are you sure?"

The Inspector's mouth flattened into a grim line. "I'm sure."

For the first time, he suspected that the Department Head was a longtime Cancer. A piece of the puzzle suddenly fell into place: his boss was the one who'd stepped in to save the Secretary from a prison sentence. He'd overlooked the multiplying books in his library. He'd even transferred him to the Inspection Department so he could meet the bookseller, the woman who had told him not to worry about his superior. Was he the one who had erased his face from the surveillance cameras those late nights at the Authority and the Labyrinth? All the prosecutor had against him were witness statements, but no recordings, not a single one. If this was the case, then the Department Head knew he wanted his daughter back, and that he wouldn't hesitate to turn any Cancers over to the authorities.

"I need a truck," he said, keeping a wary eye on the Department Head as he picked up the phone to call the police. His boss had no choice, and neither did he. In just a few minutes, a vehicle was waiting for him, as well as a police squad complete with two officers wearing black. He drove ahead of them, leading the way. His heart was pounding, throwing itself against the walls of his chest in protest.

He decided to shut off his emotions, to do whatever it took. He didn't have the luxury of thinking deeply about his actions. He would prove his loyalty, and he'd do it willingly. He had chosen to side with the government—now there was no question about his identity. And if a hookah-smoking caterpillar asked him who he was, he'd know what to say: he was a Book Censor, a Bookstore Inspector, an upright citizen in Big Brother's republic.

Most importantly, he was a father.

He told himself that after this mission, the metaphors would stop sprouting in his head. Those things only happened to readers, and starting today, he would never read again. He wouldn't be a thought criminal. And if a random figure of speech happened to spring up in his mind, he would pluck it out like a weed. *But that's a figure of speech too—I'm sliding down the slippery slope of doublethink again.* Somehow, though, he believed the symptoms of interpretation would clear up on their own, that he would be cured, that language would spit him out onto its smooth, sterile surface. And if he returned to his old position as a gatekeeper, a guardian of superficialities, then the rabbits would disappear and the world would go back to how it used to be—clean and uncomplicated.

When the court found out that it was his efforts as an inspector that had led to the arrest of a banned-books trader, a wretched bookseller, a committed Cancer—not to mention the confiscation of thousands of books concealed in a murky basement—he would immediately be deemed a respectable citizen, above all suspicion. Newspapers would write about him: INSPECTOR CONFISCATES THOUSANDS OF BANNED BOOKS FROM A HIDDEN CELLAR!

He parked next to the paint-daubed wall, in front of the jacket-clad rabbit with the pocket watch. "Take a good look at me, old man," he seethed.

Holding the green violations file and making a show of his blue uniform, he walked ahead of the two police officers and four laborers from the transport crew.

"This way, quietly please. We don't want any accidents or runaways." He could feel his chest puffing up with the pride of a hero. They were hanging on his every word, following his orders.

Pointing to the crab insignia on the wall, he said, "It's a resistance cell," as if it weren't obvious. "Pay attention, the whole area needs to be searched, but my authority begins and ends with that bookstore."

With large strides he moved toward the entrance, breathless. For the first time, he felt that the "Keep Out" on the doormat was meant for him.

He glanced at the pots of lettuce as seven white rabbits scurried out of his way. The same rabbits that used to follow him, chase him, call out to him, were fleeing, disappearing into the narrow paths that led off the alleyway.

The little bells tinkled as he pushed the door open, then he heard the bookseller's voice. "Welcome, Inspector. I've been waiting for you."

A mysterious smile played on her lips. She put her pen down—she'd been writing—then held out her hands, wrists together. He looked away. She'd known he was coming, but she hadn't tried to escape. Had the Department Head warned her he was on his way? With a nod, he motioned to the police officer to cuff her. There. It was done. And now all he wanted was for this to be over.

The bookseller didn't stop smiling. He caught a whiff of her perfume when she briefly stood next to him, her wrists stretched out to the police. *Why isn't she angry with me? Or screaming "Traitor" right here in front of everyone? Why hasn't she told the police I'm a renegade Cancer? A small, insignificant Cancer, but still a Cancer by all counts. Why isn't she exposing me?*

She gazed at him tenderly, her eyes shining with tears, as if what he'd become was understandable—no, as if it had been inevitable, a matter of fate—and that she'd known it would happen. *She must have meant what she said: she was always waiting for me.* The Inspector made it a point not to look at her, in spite of the pain clawing at his chest. He found himself comparing one pain to another. *Take the bookseller and give me back my daughter.* A police officer led her to the car outside, while he guided the rest of the men to the basement's trapdoor. "The banned material is down there." *Below the surface,* he thought of adding, but didn't. He gestured to the transport crew. "Move all the books into the truck and take them to the warehouse."

Off to the Book Detention Center, to the Labyrinth, to hell. All those books that had ruined his life. *They can have them all.* Still standing among the workers, he held his head high.

He went down to the basement and pointed at the bookshelves. But when one of the workers reached for his personal copy of *Zorba the Greek* and tossed it into a black plastic bag, he heard a crack. He felt as if his own spine had snapped. A cacophony of screaming seemed to come from the books: men's voices and women's and children's. The workers took *Alice in Wonderland* too, and *Pinocchio,* but no one noticed that other book—the king of all banned books—because its cover had been removed a long time ago. He knew perfectly well whose picture had been on the cover; it was the same one that made his daughter scream. He stood there frozen. Silenced. Trapped. It was over now. He'd done it.

But why were these metaphors still cropping up in his head? Why did it hurt him that he'd done what he had to do? When one of the transport crew noticed the tears in his eyes, he claimed it was allergies from the dust. When they'd cleared out the place entirely, after hours of sweaty work, he felt dead inside, meaningless—just like any other good citizen. He climbed back up to find the workers confiscating papers the bookseller had been writing on. They were neatly stacked, one over the other, and fastened at the top with two binder clips. It was a finished manuscript, ready for publication. Stuck on the front was a slip of paper inscribed: "To the Respected Inspector." The workers drew his attention to the note, but he dismissed them with an angry wave. He wouldn't read a single word the bookseller had written. He wouldn't read anything else, either.

"Put it with the rest of the banned materials," he said. He didn't need to inspect this particular book. He knew the woman who'd written it. He'd already condemned her to her fate.

He walked out of the bookstore. At the entrance, not a single rabbit remained. He stopped, unable to move, staring blankly at the security staff sealing the door with red wax and cordoning off the place with yellow tape. One of the workers reached out and gently tapped his shoulder, while a second man held out a sheet of paper, politely asking him to "Sign here, Inspector."

This was it, then.

He had transformed, officially, from suspect to national hero. The court would sympathize with him because he'd seized thousands of forbidden books. *So why are my limbs trembling?* He was in danger of crumpling to the ground when he thought of his daughter. His daughter who was locked away in a rehabilitation center. He signed the report.

The men shook his hand and seemed ready to hoist him up on their shoulders.

"We got these books just in time!"

"What do you mean?"

"Have you forgotten, sir? It's Purification Day!"

The Pyre.

He had forgotten about it completely.

4

YOU ARE EMPTY and meaningless, and it's for your own good to stay that way.

This time, as he spoke to himself, the voice inside him sounded like the First Censor.

You must deaden yourself. It's best if you don't feel anything at all. Don't think about the little one or the books. Go home and go to sleep. The lawyer will take care of the rest.

He didn't know what hurt more: losing his daughter, or the fact that he'd betrayed himself. All the way home, he could hear the muffled screams from the black plastic bags full of books. Because of him, more than ten thousand volumes had been impounded, which meant the empty shelves left by the books that would be burned tonight—on Purification Day—were already full again. Not to mention the bookseller, who had accepted her fate as if she'd been expecting it. Was it guilt that had made her surrender her wrists to the handcuffs and go calmly to the police station from where she'd surely disappear completely? No one would know what had become of her, just like what had happened with the old man. It was as if they had vanished at the end of a tunnel, or a black hole had swallowed them up. Perhaps it was still possible to travel through time outside of stories. He wasn't sure anymore, but where did all the prisoners go?

On arriving home, he sat in his car staring at the square building with its tiny windows and found himself unable to face the vacuum his daughter had left behind. He couldn't watch as his wife cleaned dishes till her skin peeled. He couldn't open the little girl's empty wardrobe, devoid of princess costumes, uninhabited by a single imaginary wolf.

She would be back soon, he assured himself. She had to be, now that he'd done what he'd done. The all-powerful, all-knowing government would see to it that his heroic act was rewarded. His daughter would return any day now. He leaned his head against the seat of the car and closed his eyes. What was he going to do, stuck waiting like this? Where could he go that wouldn't be painful? Where could a person hide from his wife's accusing eyes?

If only the old man hadn't been so foolish. If only they hadn't caught him reading *Pinocchio*. If only he—the Censor—had never been made a bookstore inspector. Or met the bookseller. Or found out about the Labyrinth and the Pyre. If only he'd never read *Zorba* in the first place. If only he wasn't such a chameleon: a book censor, a reader, a guardian of surfaces, a guardian of the library, a bookstore inspector, a Cancer, a hero . . . If only he knew who he was. If only the books gave him something other than questions.

What now?

He put the car back into gear and turned it toward a place he knew well, driven by an urge he couldn't explain. He would go to the Labyrinth—he could simply waltz in: the triumphant inspector. There, he wouldn't have to think about how long he would have to wait. He could lose himself completely.

5

HE FOUND HIMSELF surrounded by trucks loaded with electronics, stalls selling fancy costumes, wooden figures in human form, and a large pile of dummy books for fuel. People had come out of their homes in outfits covered with ruffles and flounces, their faces plastered in makeup. None of them were wearing khaki: their clothes sparkled in royal blues, bold reds, and fluorescent yellows. Playing musical instruments that they'd made from household utensils, they headed—some on foot, others in vehicles—to the car cemetery. It was Purification Day, and everyone wanted to watch the plays, enjoy the acrobats and clowns, and visit the open-air museums displaying cell phones, digital cameras, and compact discs. Out of all the devices, he had once most admired the portable memory sticks. But nothing impressed him anymore.

Revelers donned ghost masks and shoes that curled up at the toes like the ones worn by witches and genies. They looked like characters who'd finally broken free from the text. Kiosks sold ice cream, caramel apples, popcorn, and grilled corn on the cob. Vendors touted colorful socks adorned with smiling red flowers and fluffy white sheep on sky blue backgrounds. There was music, too, incomprehensible, with no instructive purpose such as dying for the sake of the nation.

Everyone was waiting, of course, for the show. Egged on by clamoring crowds, seven effigies would be thrown onto an enormous bonfire. He remembered the pile of fake books, too. The smell of kerosene stung his nose and he saw the fire flare, the glow of its sparkling flames reflected in thousands of eyes. The spectators cheered along. With every effigy thrown into the fire, the cheers would grow louder, until—when the final figure had been hurled into the flames—everyone was purified. They would slip out of their flamboyant clothes, wipe the makeup from their faces, and sing the anthems of the Revolution, rejoicing in the rebirth of their civilization.

The government still relied on this ritual, and every year it boosted the people's faith in the New World's principles. But he knew now that real books weren't burned in a festive atmosphere—they were quietly lit ablaze in the sprawling dirt lot in front of the strange pyramidal structure where the Labyrinth was, barely a mile from here. Time and again, he found himself pondering the government's ability to create allegories and act as if they were real. And when his thoughts took him this far astray, he began to wonder if the government believed—even more than the opposition did—in the power of imagination.

Well, they could imagine themselves into oblivion. The government and the opposition. He was going to get his daughter back.

He arrived at the dirt lot, and this time there was no reason to hide. He parked at the main entrance and walked past the workers lighting the fire in front of the building. The stench of kerosene hit him again, and he saw a team of men from the Censorship Authority and laborers from the transport crew stacking books into a pyramid, ready for burning.

The workers looked at him questioningly. He told them he was the bookstore inspector who'd reported the last batch of books. "Ten thousand titles," he said. "I wanted to stop by the warehouse. See how everything's going."

The men shrugged and went back to piling books. No one bothered to give him directions to the basement, as if it was quite normal for him to know his way there. *I'm a good citizen, above all suspicion. I could skewer the System between the eyes and I'd still be untouchable.* He walked through the front door, right in front of the surveillance cameras. It wasn't the time of day when the System was usually hacked—he knew that—and no one would erase his face from the recordings. But it didn't matter. Who would dare approach him after what he'd just pulled off? He needed to get to the Labyrinth.

6

IN A NARROW GAP between the spindly columns of books, the never-ending Towers of Babel, the man lay down on his back and closed his eyes, waiting for the Labyrinth to work its magic. What if none of what happened had actually happened? As he played the story back in his mind, there wasn't a single chapter he didn't regret. He'd been stricken by a mania for meaning, and he couldn't carry on. *How would things be different if I hadn't begun to read?*

"Boss!" It was that voice: hoarse, splintered, coming from somewhere between the books. Opening his eyes, he lifted his head toward the sound. The Keeper was standing in front of him. "What've you done?" he cried.

The caretaker's face was red, his eyes bloodshot, and his feet—of course—were bare. His headcloth was draped round his shoulders, and he'd neglected to button his shirt, leaving his potbelly and boxer shorts partly exposed. He'd always been odd, but now he was clearly distraught.

The man didn't know what to say. Should he apologize or

yell back at the Keeper? He'd been waiting for the Labyrinth to numb his pain, hoping to fade into the woodwork, but the Keeper had appeared out of nowhere.

"What are you doing here?" the Keeper demanded.

"What does it look like I'm doing?" He laid his head on the floor again, closed his eyes, and exhaled. "I'm resting."

The strange hulk of a man suddenly bellowed and pounced. Clutching the man's shirt at the shoulders, the Keeper shook him, banging his head on the floor. "You rat! You reported us!"

The room was spinning. The man managed to grab both sides of the Keeper's unbuttoned shirt. "If you don't shut up, I'll turn you in as well," he hissed.

"You betrayed the books."

"The books betrayed me!"

"You turned on the bookseller."

"Screw the bookseller."

"And Geppetto—you sold out the old man!"

He was taken aback. "What did you say?"

"I said you sold—"

"Did you say Geppetto? Was that his name?"

"Are you that stupid?"

He kicked the caretaker off, jumped up, and began to run through the matrix of book towers spread out ahead of him. One room led to another in a seemingly endless maze. After many twists and turns, he arrived at the metal staircase in the corner of the Labyrinth and hurried to the top.

The caretaker chased after him, yelling, "What happened?"

He needed to know where the workers had put the shipment of books he'd confiscated from the bookstore.

"I need my books!"

"Which books?"

"The ones they brought in today. Where are they?"

"Follow me," said the caretaker. The man led him to a pile of boxes and black plastic bags. "The new arrivals," he said, his voice heavy.

The man bent over the bags, tearing them open with his teeth, looking for that book, that name . . . There it was. *The Adventures of Pinocchio.*

He opened the first page to an illustration of a carpenter with dozens of clocks on the wall behind him, an old man busy making a boy-puppet. Pointing at the picture, he began to giggle. *Did the child know this all along?* He dissolved into hysterical laughter. "I get it! I get it!" he gasped, laughing until his ribs ached as if they might break. His guts felt as though they were about to spill out as he bent forward, arms crossed over his belly, moaning. And laughing. And weeping.

"Brother? Are you okay?" the caretaker whispered.

He raised his head toward the Keeper's voice and giggled. Then he jumped up and darted between the columns of books, shedding his clothes as he went. Shirt, pants, shoes, socks, underwear—he tossed each of them into the air, shrieking, "Damn you, old man! Goddamn you!"

"Gone off the deep end," murmured the Keeper.

But he just splayed his arms like a seagull flying over an island, dancing naked between the banned books, repeating, "I get it! I get it!"

"What do you get?"

How could he explain what he'd understood? He couldn't find the words, and dancing wasn't enough. Arms outspread, his body trembled, twisting and jerking like a slaughtered chicken.

"You can't ban imagination, no matter what you do." The old man's voice rang out inside of him. "You'll never be able to stop it. It'll swell up and start pumping its offspring into the world, one after the other: Geppetto, Alice, Big Brother, Zorba . . . Bastards of the imagination, one and all, born of the forbidden world, even if they forget—or pretend to forget—where they came from."

He slapped his own face, again and again. His body seemed to have a mind of its own, twirling and leaping, his feet barely touching the floor. He threw back his head and guffawed. *They would come and demand what they wanted from you: They wanted you to believe in them! Imagination is real. Reality is imagined. And that wretched old man, why didn't he tell me who he was? I should have known!*

"Brother?"

He looked at the Keeper as if seeing him for the first time. "I know you," he muttered.

He gazed at the sailor with the sunburned face and the massive forearms, the great dancer on the beach. His head began to swim and the floor swayed under his feet. He steadied himself on a nearby column of books.

"Tell me, Zorba," he said, "which one of us is real and which one is imaginary? I was the one who brought you here, wasn't I? I read your book dozens of times, until you couldn't ignore me anymore. Did you come here just for me, Zorba?"

Bizarre images crowded his mind. If this was Zorba, what about the Department Head? And the President—why did he look like Big Brother? And what about his daughter?

The dizziness grew stronger and, eyes closed, he sank to his knees and slumped his head against the books lined up in front of him. He wailed, banging his head against the shelf. "Where's my daughter? Where is she?"

He saw the Keeper moving away and sat up. "Hey, Zorba!" he called. "Where are you going?" But the man didn't answer. He walked until he disappeared, his footsteps fading into silence.

Crushed, the man rose and scurried after the Keeper. Perhaps he too could reach the place where all the others came from: the old man, Zorba, Big Brother, the rabbits—and perhaps his daughter? Perhaps there, on the other side of the line between reality and imagination, their pain would no longer exist. But he lost his way. The Labyrinth swallowed him up completely, and he found himself scrambling in circles, crying out for Zorba. Men's voices drifted to him from the far end of the building.

"Where'd Montag go?" someone called. He ran toward the voices and saw the workers whose shirts reeked of kerosene. They'd lit the Purification Pyre and were here for more books. They were collecting the books that had just been seized.

"No! No! Not those!" he shouted. "Those are new books! Put them down!"

One of them held a copy of *Zorba the Greek*. He snatched the book out of the man's hand. "Take some other books!"

"What the hell? What are you doing, man?" the worker snapped. "And why are you naked?"

"Looks like he's not all there," another said derisively.

"These books aren't due to be burned yet. They still have a whole year to go!"

"Definitely a crackpot," the workers muttered, shaking their heads. Carrying empty boxes, they moved deeper into the Labyrinth, reaching for random books and tossing them into boxes.

Where had Zorba gone? Could the intelligence services torture a character from a book? What if this pain wasn't real?

His knees gave way and he fell backward onto a mound of books. As he lay on the contraband that he himself had impounded, he felt something sharp poking into his bare back. He reached beneath him and pulled out a clipped stack of papers.

The manuscript written by the bookseller.

On the first page, the title: *The Book Censor's Library*.

Ha! He'd known all along she was writing about him! Maybe she was in love with him after all. Well, she could rot in the cells of the secret police forever.

He turned the page and read:

As the Book Censor awoke one morning, filled with others' words, he found himself transformed into a reader.

7

THE MAN SAT cross-legged on the pile of books he'd confiscated, engrossed in the bookseller's manuscript. Everything he read, he already knew: from the moment he'd fallen into the trap of meaning until now. He sat, bare as the day he was born, reading the story of his life.

Is that why she was smiling? Because I myself am unreal?

Three workers walked by, carrying a box of books.

"Hey guys!"

They turned to look at him: stark naked, grinning like a lunatic.

"I'm a character in a book!"

Their eyes filled with alarm, or was it pity? "We should call the police," one of them said.

At the bottom of the page he held in his hands, he read: "I'm a character in a book!"

8

EVERYTHING he'd lived through—every rib-shattering blow, every metaphor that had sprouted in his head, every voice that had sprung from his depths—was there in the manuscript. The bookseller had written it all down. His story as he knew it.

Had the events in his life unfolded as she wrote them? Or had she always been one step ahead? She had stopped writing at the exact moment he'd stepped into the bookstore to arrest her. She had known what was going to happen. And now, with saintly generosity, she was giving him a chance to discover his fate. But he didn't understand what made a writer decide to give up her life for one of her characters. Why had she allowed him to hand her over to the authorities? If it was her will behind everything that had happened, where was his own will? And if the bookseller had written him, who had written the bookseller? Who had written the writer who'd written the bookseller? He didn't understand why she'd tormented him so cruelly, why'd she'd created such a place, emptied it of all meaning, and then forced him to endure existence there.

And if his fate was written in this manuscript, was it possible for him to go off-script? The bookseller could drop dead for all he cared. Only one thing mattered now: to find out what happened next.

He turned the page.

His heart nearly burst from his chest.

He began to pant as he read.

The court had ruled in his favor after the arrest of the bookseller and the seizure of thousands of banned books. Even the lawyer hadn't expected the scales to tip so heavily in his favor. After further investigation, the authorities arrested the Department Head, who was discovered to be involved with a cell of Cancers. The First Censor was promoted to Department Head. And the seven censors became six.

And even though his daughter's case was advanced and difficult to treat, the medical report had concluded that biological—not environmental—factors were to blame for her condition. The System couldn't punish a good citizen for the mistakes of nature. In the court's opinion, it was in the child's best interest for her father to visit her at the center. Such a visit would have a positive effect while she was reeducated to abide by the values of society and the aspirations of the New World.

His heart pounded harder. He was going to see his daughter again, even if it was in the pages of a book. Taking a deep breath, he read on.

9

WHEN HE REACHED the rehabilitation center, the man found his daughter tied to the bed with leather straps, her eyelids taped open, forcing her to look at the screen on the ceiling.

There were pictures of the President everywhere: on the ceiling, on the wall opposite the bed, and at intervals on either side of the corridors. Being surrounded by images of the President would speed up recovery, the nurse told him. His heart grew heavy. His daughter wasn't kicking and screaming. Deprived even of the right to close her eyes, she lay listless, her gaze fixed on the President. He was glad his wife was not with him. Her wails would have brought down the roof, and the center might have barred them from visiting again. He couldn't help thinking of the goldfinch in its cage, its cover blown off.

"Do you need anything else?" asked the nurse. He shook his head, and she stepped out into the corridor.

He moved closer to his daughter, the strength draining from his legs as he saw the wires fixed to her body, the buds in her ears, the machines monitoring her vital signs.

"I'm here, my love," he said.

But his daughter didn't appear to recognize him or respond to his voice. He reached out and waved a hand in front of her eyes. *Can she even see?* He laid his palm over her eyes to rest them and a tear slipped down his face. He took out her earbuds and whispered, "Shall I tell you a story?" One good story would make her feel better, and he knew a great one.

"Once upon a time, there was a grandma who lived inside a wolf's belly. The wolf lived in a little girl's wardrobe. When the wolf ate the grandma, she tasted delicious because of all the stories she knew, like the one about the magic mirror, and the pretty woman who came out of a lemon, and the genie in the bottle, and the old man with the boy-puppet."

She moved her lips as if she was trying to say something. But no words came out. She had forgotten them all.

Broken, he rested his head on the edge of the bed, trying to conceal his sobs.

He looked at the straps fixing her tiny body to the bed, the welts on her wrists and ankles. *Why have they tied her up like a dangerous criminal when she's only a child?* He reached out and loosened the straps, massaged the welts on her skin, kissed her fingers, one by one.

And then the nurse came and escorted him out.

10

THE NEXT DAY, he received a summons from the rehabilitation center. When he arrived, he was not taken to see his daughter but directed to an investigation room.

An officer was already seated with a sheet of paper on his desk. Though he was afraid to ask, he drew up his courage. "Where's my daughter?"

The officer said nothing. He merely pushed the sheet of paper toward him.

It had happened last night.

The leather straps that tied the child to the bed were loose, the report said, and investigators were still working to hold the responsible party accountable.

His daughter had freed herself and slipped out of bed. Because of the limited number of staff on the night shift, no one had noticed. Like the goldfinch that flung itself against the bars of its cage, she had begun to hit her head against the wall at the exact spot where the picture of the President hung. Again and again and again.

11

IN THE DIRT LOT outside the Labyrinth, the Purification bonfire's flames reached higher into the sky. Thousands of books had already been thrown to their end, their covers flapping frantically like the wings of injured pigeons until they *went up in sparkling whirls and blew away on a wind turned dark with burning*. The smell of kerosene filled the air. A row of fire extinguishers stood sentry in the sand, waiting patiently for the last book to burn.

That afternoon, workers had been startled by the sight of a naked man running out of the building. Wild-eyed, he raved that nothing was real, that nothing had happened. No one was sure who he was. One of the workers tried to approach and ask him, but the man broke down in giggles—he couldn't for the life of him come up with an answer.

Someone rushed to find a cloth to cover him as the man looked at the Purification fire, an incandescent smile on his face. "I've discovered—" he said. Then he broke out in a mad dash, evading the workers' grasp. A split second later he jumped into the blaze.

The laborers erupted into panicked shouting. They raced for the extinguishers and sprayed streams of white foam into the raging flames.

When the fire finally receded, they could find no trace of the man's body.

Had he even existed?

Or had he just been a character in a book?